# The Haunting Of Larkspur Farm

## The Hauntings Of Kingston Book 4

### Michelle Dorey

# ABOUT THIS BOOK

Larkspur Farm is the refuge which Paige and her family have longed for. A hobby farm in the countryside is a welcome change from the congestion and crime of big city life. Now hopefully, her sister Amanda can recover from her clinical depression and resume being the mother she was before, to her two young children. It better work because the family has sunk every penny to make this new life work.

But from the day they move in, their welcome to the new home is plagued with a series of eerie events--events that seem innocent in the beginning; that photo in the living room just won't stay straight!

But the picture's only the beginning...when Paige discovers an antique music box, malevolent spirits stir. Skeptical at first, Paige becomes intrigued, then alarmed. When she discovers the farm's tragic past, she's horrified.

They all become terrified as the mysteries of Larkspur Farm are revealed. They're not the newest owners of Larkspur Farm. They're its latest victims.

Larkspur Farm doesn't want them to keep its secrets.

It wants them dead.

# Contents

To my Mother and Father—I think of you every day.

# CHAPTER ONE

P aige cringed when she saw the door open and Jennifer emerge from the old lady's den. Oh shit. It was her turn now.

Silently cursing the fact that she hadn't been able to dodge this bullet, she got to her feet. But really, what could she say? It was Jennifer's birthday wish and how often do you turn twenty-five, a quarter of a century? Her friend's blue eyes were sparking with excitement after hearing what the old biddy had 'seen' in her fortune.

Paige watched Jennifer plop down next to Alison on the ancient, over-stuffed sofa, the two of them already talking a mile a minute past each other, extolling the predictions of Lady Mystical. The pizza they'd shared at the birthday supper took a slow roll in Paige's stomach and she toyed with the idea of rushing out of the shoddy townhouse.

Jennifer looked up for a moment and broke off mid sentence from her conversation with Alison. "You okay, Paige?" Without waiting for a response, she grinned and continued, "Seriously...it's fun. I can't wait to hear what she tells *you*."

Paige's fingers closed over the glass doorknob, her eyes barely registering the brown, crackled varnish of the door. She took a deep breath before turning it and stepping inside. Filmy blue eyes stared out from a heart shaped face, the skin as fine and delicate as parchment, while a nest of silver hair topped the elderly lady's small head. There was a knowing, enigmatic smile on her thin lips while her eyes seemed to bore right through Paige, sending a chill up her spine.

"Come in, dear. Have a seat." One of the woman's blue veined hands left the deck of cards, gesturing at the chair across from her. "This won't take long. Don't worry."

Paige hesitated, looking down at the spindly chair with the needlepoint floral seat. For a second, she saw herself as the old lady must be viewing her—a smart-assed millennial, eager to appease her friends and get this over with. Well in that, the woman definitely showed a degree of clairvoyance.

She swallowed hard and eased down into the chair. Actually, this kind of stuff scared her more than she would ever admit. Even her sister didn't know about the premonitions she'd had on that nightmare of days—the day their parents were killed in the car accident. She'd been a basket case, alternating between crying and silent dread, knowing something bad was going to happen, but no details as to what that thing would be.

And now, here she was about to delve into that spooky stuff again with a stranger. Please God, don't let this woman bring up the death of her parents. Even though it was now more than three years in the past, the wound still felt raw.

Madam Mystical picked up the heavy glass holder containing a bundle of spindly, smoldering weed and circled the deck of large cards with it, letting the smoke drift in a swirl over the table.

The pungent smell filled Paige's nostrils and she eased back in her chair from her rigid perch on the edge.

The old lady set the smudge aside and her gaze linked with Paige's. "The tarot cards tap into universal energy, which of course, includes your own energy." She set her elbows on the table and folded her hands together, resting her chin on them, silently staring at Paige. The only sound was the grandfather clock in the corner of the room, ticking like a time bomb.

Paige's lips parted and she peered with narrow eyes at the old woman. "What's wrong? Shouldn't you be—"

"Silence."

Paige jerked back and her mouth closed with a snap. What the heck? This wasn't going the way she'd pictured a psychic reading, nothing like what Hollywood hype portrayed. The watery gleam in the old woman's eyes staring intently made Paige's neck muscles seize up tight as a fist.

The old woman sniffed and sat back in her chair, resting her gnarled fingers once more on the table. "With you, a simple three card reading will suffice." She nodded to the stack of cards in the centre of the table. "Think of something in your life that you are unsure of...a question about your family, a lover or even your job. Shuffle the deck seven times while pondering your question."

Paige reached for the cards, holding them for a beat while her mind flashed to her sister. She was the only family left. Poor Amanda. How many times had Paige visited her sister in the three years since Avril was born, only to find her crying in bed? The term 'post partum depression' didn't come close to describing the black hopelessness her sister had suffered. And just when she was coming out of it, she'd had to deal with the death of their parents.

It had been hard for both of them but more so for Amanda. Paige could still see her sister's frail body propped up by Josh's strong arm as they walked from the grave, a broken woman.

Paige's eyes narrowed and her teeth clenched thinking of the final straw, the one that threw Amanda back down into the depths of depression just as she seemed to be getting better. The cops still hadn't caught the punks who had broken into Amanda and Josh's home and trashed it, taking only a laptop.

She shuffled the cards, seeing her sister's tear-filled grey eyes, her fingers clutching her arms, wringing the flesh while Josh cradled their two kids in his burly grasp, glaring at the wreckage the hoodlums had caused in his home. The family sure as hell hadn't needed that. And such a setback for Amanda.

Paige had spent every day off and even some sick time trying to help out with the kids, keep the household running while Amanda alternated between sleeping and crying herself to sleep.

At first, Paige's boss had been patient but that was wearing thin too. She swallowed hard thinking of the letter she'd been given—the letter threatening dismissal for absenteeism. They needed someone reliable to show up for work at the group home.

"Cut the cards three times, setting them in three stacks. Take the top card from each stack and place it face up in front of you. The first card represents your past. The second card, the present and the third card, your future." The old lady's voice was faint, barely above a whisper, and her eyes were intent watching her.

Paige's fingers trembled a little as she set the cards down and divided them into three separate piles. She barely dared to breath in the suddenly thick air, while the candle's light flickered wildly on the sideboard.

The first card showed a young man in armor astride a horse, holding a golden, star shaped pentacle in his hand. The Knight of Pentacles was printed at the bottom. At the sight of the five-pointed star, her stomach did a flip flop.

She plucked the top card from the middle pile and flipped it over, setting it next to the first. Her eyes became wide and she jerked back. The card showed a young family, the kingly father reaching down to play with a child at his feet while behind him a blond-haired woman smiled down at them. In her arms was a bunch of red roses. Bordering the edges of the scene were ten of the same pentacles that the knight in the first card carried.

It could have been Amanda and Josh in the card's picture! But, not exactly as there wasn't a baby and they sure as heck didn't live in a castle, but still…

She took a breath and let it out slowly before reaching for the last card and flipping it over. This was the one that represented her future. When she turned it over and set it next to the other two, her hand held the corner, frozen in place. There was a stone tower being struck by lightning, fire erupting from its windows while a young person fell to the ground. Oh shit, that couldn't be good. A shiver skittered down her spine.

She bit her lower lip and looked up at the old lady, trying to read her face. But aside from the set line of her lips and eyes flickering from card to card, there was no clue what she thought.

Lady Mystical sat straight and folded her hands in front of her. "The Knight of Pentacles representing your past, shows a person who is steady, and patient. Someone who has worked hard to achieve her goals."

Paige nodded and then caught herself, sitting up straighter and trying to maintain a poker face. The old lady smiled and looked down at the cards once more.

"Your present…hmmm…there is family involved." Her eyes flickered up for a moment, "I see success. However, there are many burdens, hardships involved with this success." Her head tilted to the side and she squinted, gazing hard at Paige. "You are not married. This is not your child nor husband."

Paige's stomach roiled at the old woman's words. This was hitting things right on the mark.

The old woman sat back and her eyebrows rose. "It is hardship for you, I think. This card in conjuncture with the Knight denotes that. It speaks to your character and resilience. But there is more…much more, I'm afraid." She folded her hands in front of her, staring hard across the table. "Are you sure you would like me to go on?"

Paige's heart thumped hard in her chest and she rubbed her sweaty palms over the threadbare denim on her thighs. She nodded, not trusting herself to speak.

"There is danger around you. Do you know about protecting yourself from spiritual forces?"

Paige's mouth became dry and she barely dared to breathe. The old woman's tone had become earnest, her ancient eyes staring intently into Paige's. She shook her head. "I don't know what you are talking about. This is—"

The old woman slapped the table with her hand and leaned forward. "I know you have the sixth sense. I knew it the moment you walked through the door. You foresaw the death of two people you were very close to. And, I know it wasn't that long ago." The old lady took a deep breath and closed her eyes for a moment before continuing.

"You also sense spirits. You were visited by your deceased grandmother when you were a little girl. Isn't that right?"

Paige felt her throat grow tight while her eyes welled with tears. This wasn't fair. None of it was. That drunk driver ramming into her parents' car...Amanda's depression and then those punks breaking in... Shit! And now to sit here and re-live the nightmares, worry about some kind of '*danger*' and protecting herself?

She took a deep breath and shook her head sharply to dispel the tears. "Look, I've had some weird things happen. Who hasn't? Not sure that means I should protect myself, whatever that entails." She tapped her finger a few times on the last card. "What about this one? The one that's supposed to be my future. What does it have to do with that? Tell me."

"There are forces, unnatural forces that are aligning against you. The time we live in is precarious. We are on the brink of world war...possibly. If not that, then climate disasters that we've never seen the likes of. The veil that keeps dark forces at bay is growing thin."

She reached across and her bony fingers clutched Paige's arm. "You will experience malevolent entities, but you must protect yourself first before you can help your family. There are charms, amulets and even the way you must guard your thoughts, when you're in the presence of..." She sighed. "...of evil entities."

An icy chill swept through Paige's body and she shuddered. The sight of the card, the lightning striking it and the body falling to its death shot a bolt of fear through her heart. Her eyes locked with the old woman's and the look of alarm she saw made her blood run cold.

"How am I supposed to do that? I don't even know who or what my enemy is. You say evil entities, but how am I to know them? What are you really saying?" Paige's eyes welled with tears but this time from anger.

She was only in her mid twenties, just starting to carve out a place for herself...with every spare minute helping her sister cope. And now this witch was warning of evil entities out to get her? It was too much!

She shrugged the woman's hand off and stood up so fast the chair toppled backward, landing with a soft thud on the worn carpet. "This is bullshit."

She scrambled in her purse with trembling fingers, trying to locate her wallet. Her fingers closed around it, snatched a twenty from the soft leather and she plunked it sharply onto the table, upsetting the third stack of cards.

"Here! Thanks for the reading. It was entertaining—NOT!" As she turned, her eye paused on the card that had spilled from the deck, facing up and accusing her. It was a man hanging by one leg, upside down from a cross, while a halo of golden light circled his head. 'The Hanged Man' was inscribed on the bottom.

The old woman stared at the card, then back up to Paige. "You're coming to a crossroad, my dear," was all she said.

Paige spun on her heels and fled from the room.

# CHAPTER TWO

## *A week later...*

Paige's hands drifted softly over her niece's back and she leaned down to sniff the toddler's downy hair. There was nothing sweeter than the scent of Avril's skin and hair just fresh from the bath. She pulled the three-year-old in closer and crossed her legs, adjusting the child's weight against her body.

Across the table, Amanda's eyes were bright and her smile a mile wide, leaning forward in her chair. Despite the fact that she was in her thirties, with a few lines crossing her forehead, she looked young, excited as a kid on Christmas morning.

"Oh my God, Paige! Wait till you see it. The house needs a little work, decorating mainly—nothing drastic or structural. And the barn! I'll be able to get a couple horses and maybe some chickens and—"

Josh slapped the table. "Hold on!" He shook his head, but his eyes were crinkled in laughter.

For a moment the smile fell from Amanda's face and even the sleepy black dog laying next to Josh rose to its feet.

Amanda huffed a sigh. "What? You know I want to get back into animal care. It's a hobby farm, a perfect set-up for boarding and grooming. That's a big part of the appeal."

Paige's eyes locked with Josh's for a moment. She turned to her sister. "You don't want to over-extend yourself though, Sis. Moving to the co untry...hell, another city is going to be a huge adjustment as it is." Paige's shoulders slumped. She was really going to miss them.

But, it had been a long time since she'd seen her big sister this happy. Amanda's eyes were framed in dark lashes, thickened with a brush of mascara and she even wore a trace of lipstick. Not that she needed make-up to look pretty but the fact that she was wearing it, meant the new meds were working. Her energy level and enthusiasm were really encouraging. Maybe, she truly was better now.

Josh pushed back from the table and shook his head, looking at Amanda. "I'm not saying you can't. Just not right away." He opened the fridge door and bent to grab a beer.

Paige looked over at her brother-in-law. The engineering firm where he worked didn't even have an office in Kingston. "But what about you, Josh? How are you going to manage this promotion, splitting your time between Toronto and Montreal? You're going to be on the road all the time."

He laughed and shot a smile at Amanda. "I'll manage. Kingston is the half way point between the two cities. It'll mean some driving for sure, but it beats watching her check every lock and window in the house before bed and then recheck them, *six more times*! This is crazy, living in fear. At least it's a smaller city with probably less crime. It'll be better to raise the kids there."

Amanda rolled her eyes and smiled. "Laugh all you want about my paranoia. I'm just glad we were all out that day they broke in. Thank God even Barney was at the beach with us, not here probably getting beaten or even killed."

Paige sighed. The lonesomeness that she'd tried to hide was probably showing on her face now. It wasn't just Amanda she'd miss. It was Avril and Julian, Josh and even that slobbering fool of a dog, Barney. For the past year she'd practically lived at her sister's house, helping out. It was great that Amanda looked happy again, making plans but that didn't mean when she moved, there wouldn't be a big hole in her own life.

Josh took a deep breath, and pulled his shoulders back as he stepped over behind Amanda's chair and rested his hand on her shoulder. He smiled looking over at Paige and after a brief glance up at him, Amanda turned and gazed at her sister too.

"About the new house...Paige..." Amanda leaned forward in her chair, a nervous smile spreading on her lips.

Uh oh. It was apparent she was being set up—that they had something they had talked about and were about to spring on her. "What?" She stared at Amanda, trying to read her face.

Amanda leaned forward and placed her hand on Paige's arm. "Look, it's just you and me now, Paige. With Mom and Dad gone, we need to stick together. Leaving you here is the downside of getting the farm in Kingston."

Josh cleared his throat and continued. "I'm going to be gone most of the week, living out of a suitcase, overseeing projects in Montreal and Toronto. What we're getting at..." His eyebrows rose high, "...we'd like you to come with us, Paige."

She could feel her eyes get wider and wider and her mouth fall open. "Go with you? But what about my job, my apartment?"

Amanda squeezed her arm and when she spoke there were tears glistening her eyes. "Paige, Josh told me that you got a letter of warning about all the time you took off work. It was because of me, being sick and all. So really, how secure is that job? We could pay you to help me with the kids and the farm."

Josh jumped in, "Yeah. I'll be making way more money and we're making a profit selling this house. The house in Kingston is cheap by Toronto standards."

Paige couldn't help the smile that twitched on her lips. "No."

Amanda gaped and Paige couldn't help the chuckle watching her sister's face. But crazy as it seemed, the knot in her stomach had unraveled when they asked her to go with them. There was no way she was going to say no. Plus, what was so important in Toronto that would keep her there?

She grinned, "You aren't paying me. I've got some money saved."

Amanda popped out of her chair and clasped Paige's shoulders, planting a big kiss on her forehead. "Oh thank goodness! The kids would have been heartbroken if you weren't there, not to mention us." She pulled back and looked at Avril, snuggled in Paige's arms. She nodded and reached for her, lifting the sleeping child up.

When she left the kitchen, Josh took a seat at the table. "She's really perked up with this move, Paige. The meds have helped but I think getting her out of the city is the real deal." He looked down at the bottle of beer and his fingernail scraped at the edge of the label, prying it loose. "Still...I know I'll feel better having you there. Julian has another year till he's in school and as for Avril...Well, it's a lot for Amanda. She's still kind of rocky, and having a three-year-old and a five-year-old to look after is a bit much right now. Add the getting settled into the new house..." he paused, "we really need your help."

She knew exactly what he was getting at. There'd been too many times that they'd talked together, both worried about Amanda and of course, the kids. He was going out on a limb with this, moving the family far away to a home in the country. If it didn't work out, he needed a safety net for the kids. He was counting on her to be that safety net.

Paige looked across to the family room where Julian was curled up on the sofa, sound asleep while the Disney movie he'd been watching played on. He was a little angel with Josh's curls and fair complexion.

She turned and smiled at Josh. "It's not like I have a boyfriend or anyone keeping me here. I'll come back the odd time to see Jennifer and the gang."

Josh rolled his eyes and grinned. "Yeah. It's not like you couldn't have your pick of guys. Maybe Mr. Right is living in Kingston, just waiting for you to show up."

"Hmph. I doubt it." She pictured Tony, the guy she'd wasted a year of her life on until she caught him cheating. But that had been a couple of years ago and since then, Amanda and her family had needed her. "I'll be around as long as you need me." She smiled and tapped his hand. "For what it's worth, I think she's rounded a corner in her treatment, too."

Josh chuckled. "You should know. You're the expert in this."

She shook her head. "No expert, but I know a few things about mental health after working at the group home." She gasped as another thought popped into her head. "Oh my God, when are you moving? I'll have to give notice on my apartment and at work."

"We take possession September first. So you've got two months. And... we still have to sell this house." Josh got to his feet and walked quietly over to the family room to turn the TV off.

She watched him scoop Julian into his arms and then Amanda appeared at his side. The two of them shared a sweet look and Amanda's hand rose to gently rub her son's pajama clad back. It was a warm picture of love and family, which struck a chord in Paige's mind.

Oh my God. The fortune teller...the card. The three of them were eerily familiar to the Tarot card she'd drawn, the one representing the present. And from the pictures Amanda had shown her of the farmhouse, the grey limestone, it wasn't all that different from the stone castle depicted on the card.

An acrid foul taste filled her mouth, and she pulled back in her chair. The final card revealed that day, the one with the tower being struck by lightning flashed in her mind. What were they getting into?

She chided herself and took a deep breath. There was nothing to worry about. That warning had been the exaggerated theatrics of Lady Mystical. Things would be fine.

# CHAPTER THREE

*Two months later, September 1st*

"Aunt Paige!" Julian's face lit up like fireworks before his small feet raced across the room to the front door.

Behind him, pink tongue lolling out from a wide yap, Barney loped over. The Bouvier des Flandres' heavy feet and toenails clicked the hardwood floor with each step and Paige grinned watching him. The dog had always looked cross eyed to her, with the big lock of hair falling over its forehead between the high, pointed ears.

Julian hugged her thighs and beamed a grin up at her. Paige's heart swelled with love for the small, sandy-haired tyke. She reached down and scooped him up into her arms. Now *that* was a welcome if ever there was one! She kissed his cheek and toed her sandals off, already on her way into the house.

"How's my big boy today? Where's Mommy and Daddy?" She looked into the living room as she passed, noticing the sofa and chair framed by neatly stacked, brown cardboard boxes.

"They're upstairs packing the last of Avril's stuff. Can Barney and I go with you in your car? I never get to ride in your car." He reached into her shirt pocket for her sunglasses, slipping them on his face and giving her a cheesy grin.

She stifled a laugh at the sight of his tiny face dwarfed by the dark sunglasses like some kind of giant fly. "Sure can. As long as it's okay with your Mom and Dad."

At the soft thuds of footsteps on the stairs, she turned.

"What's he talking you into now, Paige? I swear, he's got you wrapped around his finger and you love every minute of it." The smile on Amanda's face as she stepped down the stairs sent a warm feeling through Paige.

"Totally! He's my favorite nephew." She gave his cheek a big kiss.

"We won't mention that he's your *only* nephew, will we?" Amanda's eyebrows bobbed high, and it was just like old times, when she used to tease Paige, the younger, pesky sister.

Paige grinned. "He wants to ride with me. A walk on the wild side in the Miata, rather than the 'Griswold' van. Not too sure about Barney though. He'd never fit." She set Julian down and stepped over to her sister. "You two all packed up now? You really think we'll be able to stay there tonight?" Paige looked up at her sister. "It's not too late to book a hotel and tackle the unpacking and set up in the morning."

Amanda shook her head. "It's only three hours away. There'll be plenty of time this afternoon to set the beds and kitchen up. That's really all we need for tonight." She gripped Paige's forearm and squeezed it. "I can't wait to show you the place! It's like my all-time dream house! A hobby farm on a lake."

"Hi Paige. Did the movers already get your stuff?"

At the sound of Josh's voice Paige looked up at the stairs once more and smiled seeing Avril in his arms. The child's blue eyes were wide and her arms outstretched to Paige, almost squirming out of her father's burly grip. "Aunt Paige!"

She took the toddler in her arms and kissed the top of her dark head, again inhaling the innocent baby smell. "Hi Avril."

Meanwhile Julian was back tugging at the bottom of her T shirt. "C'mon Aunt Paige. Let's go."

She ruffled the boy's curly locks and turned to Josh. "The movers took everything at the apartment an hour ago. I popped in to see Jennifer before I came over. So yeah, I'm all set. It's going to be weird leaving though."

"After that break-in…" Amanda huffed a sigh as she gave the house a final once over. "I'm not going to miss living here, that's for sure." Turning to Paige, she said, "If Julian is going with you, you'll need his booster seat." She walked over to the front door and then turned, signaling for the others to follow.

Paige looked around at the living room and the dining room across from it. They'd lived there for seven years and she'd always considered it her second home. She pictured the times they'd sat around the table, the Christmas dinners and the celebrations, going back to when her parents were still alive. Amanda might be totally fine with leaving all this but there were good times too, in the beginning, before she got sick.

At Julian's tug, harder this time, she looked down and took his hand walking over to the front door. Behind her she could hear Josh's footsteps and the jangle of Barney's collar and tags as the leash was snapped on.

She turned and smiled at Josh. "This is quite the caravan we have, driving to Kingston. You know, I've never been there. Three hours away and never set foot inside the city."

Josh's smile belied the sadness in his eyes. He also gave the house a once over. "Sure, it's time to move on... but there were some pretty darn good times in this place, you know." Turning back to face her his face brightened. "As far as Kingston... well, the pace is a little slower but it's a pretty spot. You'll like it, Paige."

"I sure hope so." She led her nephew outside, where Amanda was leaning into the black Jeep unbuckling the booster seat. She glanced back at the doorway, seeing Josh shut it for the final time. Her stomach felt like a lump of lead and tears welled in her eyes suddenly. Even though it wasn't *her* house, she had spent a lot of time there. But over-riding the sadness was a sense of unease.

"Aunt Paige?"

She looked down and saw her nephew looking up at her with wide eyed concern. She took a deep breath and pulled her shoulders back, forcing a smile. This was silly. This was a new beginning not an ending. Kingston would be a fresh start.

"Sorry Julian. Got a little sad there for a moment." She handed the toddler to Josh and then bent to pick up the car seat.

The fortune teller's face flashed in her mind, along with the words she had spoken. *'Protect yourself first and then you can help the others'*. A chill skittered up Paige's spine. In all the mayhem, the packing and preparing for the move, she'd forgotten the fortune teller's warning until then. But why, now of all times, did it pop into her head?

She tried to shake the feeling of dread as she settled the booster seat in the car. The last time she'd felt this way, her parents had been killed in a car crash. All that fateful day she had been restless and teary, jumping at every little noise. She'd been at home, not at work, thank God. She could never have helped clients when she could barely keep a coherent thought in her head.

And then, the police had showed up at her door. She hadn't needed to see their somber serious faces to know the worst had happened. The most kind and loving parents a girl could ask for, gone in the blink of an eye.

And for some reason, that jittery, fearful feeling was back again.

When she turned to put Julian in the car seat, his eyes were welled up with tears. His voice was barely above a whisper. "I'm scared too, Aunt Paige."

# Chapter Four

*That afternoon...*

Ahead of her, the left turn light of Amanda's Jeep blinked, catching Paige's eye. The last hour and a half had been quiet in her tiny car, after Julian drifted off to sleep. The three-lane highway seemed to go on forever. Now, that they were on the smaller road, the last leg of the journey, she perked up.

There was so much green space, fields where herds of cows meandered, lazily munching in the afternoon sun. It was different—the air fresh, the spaces more open from what she was used to. She drove by farmhouses and barns set well back from the road. The spaces between them were long and lonely. One thing that would definitely take some getting used to would be the sense of isolation, totally unlike the cookie-cutter houses rubbing shoulders in big city.

At Amanda's brake lights ahead of her, she eased off the accelerator. They seemed to crawl at a snail's pace through the tiny village—if a gas station, a general store, a squat limestone library and a smattering of bungalows bordering the street could be considered a village.

"Are we there yet?" Julian asked.

She turned and grinned, watching him blink the sleepiness out of his eyes. "Almost, I think. We're in some place called Inverary. Your mom said the house is about ten minutes past this village."

"I thought we were going to live in Kingston," he said, peering out the window.

"This is just a village kind of on the outskirts." She grinned. "We're almost there."

"Good. I need to go to the bathroom." Proving his point, he squirmed in his seat.

"Think of something else. How about what color you want to paint your room or if there's a tree where your Dad can hang a swing, or playing in the barn, making forts in the hay. I've read about that." She smiled and punched the accelerator again, following Amanda's lead.

After a few minutes the jeep ahead signaled and turned right onto a dirt road. There was a small green sign—'Larkspur Lane' They had to be getting close now. Yellow fields of hay bordered each side of the road, while in the distance a line of trees stood like sentinels.

Julian was really squirming now, his face blank and inwardly focused. Her fingers tapped the steering wheel, watching the tail lights ahead of them.

"You okay, buddy? I can pull over and—"

"No! There's no bathroom or..." He looked at her with shock, squeezing his legs together.

At Amanda's turn-signal flashing, she smiled. "We're here buddy! You did it, Julian."

She parked the car next to Amanda's and her eyes grew wide as she looked out the windshield at the imposing two story, stone building. From the ground, thick solid walls of limestone block rose two stories. Two angled peaks broke the line of the slate gray roof, reaching upward and ending in points as sharp as spears, while under them, huddled close together, arched windows peeked out.

For an instant, there was a flash of light reflected in the window on the left. Her eyes narrowed focusing there. Was there someone in the window? She blinked hard and looked again. Maybe it was the sun appearing suddenly from the bank of clouds. Even so, the hair on the back of her neck tingled and she shuddered.

At Julian's sharp intake of breath, Paige turned to look at him. His eyes were like marbles looking up at the same window and his face was blanched of colour.

"What is it, Julian? Are you okay?"

The door next to Julian opened and Josh's face appeared, his gaze looking from Julian's eyes down to the dark, spreading wetness on the front of the boy's pants.

"I'm sorry. I couldn't hold it anymore." The boy's eyes filled with tears and his lower lip quivered watching his father.

"It's okay, Julian. You didn't mean to. It was an accident. We'll get you changed into clean pants in no time." Josh's smile was warm when he gazed at Julian and unhooked the seat belt. Julian slid by him and stood next to the car, facing away.

Josh took his son's hand and led him to the jeep, before Amanda appeared carrying Avril in her arms. Paige got out and walked over to join her.

Amanda's eyes flashed wide with surprise taking in her son and she whispered. "He wet himself? He hasn't done that since he was two years old. Not even at night!"

"He's pretty embarrassed, I think. Doing that, especially in front of me. Poor little guy." Paige couldn't help the glance up at the window where she'd seen the light flash. Whatever Julian had seen up there had spooked him as well. She'd talk to him about that later.

Amanda fished in her pocket for a moment and then held a silver key before her. "Come on! I can't wait for you to see the inside. Isn't the house gorgeous?" She set off to the steps of the wide, wrap-around veranda.

Paige hesitated a moment, watching Josh help his son into a clean pair of pants that had been packed in the Jeep. It wasn't a great introduction to their new house for the boy.

She tried to shake the knot in the back of her neck loose when she turned to follow her sister. "Yeah. It sure is big! And old. I bet this place is over a hundred years old."

Amanda pushed the door wide and stepped inside, still balancing her daughter in her arms. "At least a hundred years." She looked past Paige and set Avril down, holding her arms out to her son who raced over. "Hey Julian. Feeling better now?" She gave him a hug and then took his hand, leading him to the room on the left.

Paige looked around from the high ten foot ceilings with cove molding to the wide oak staircase in front of her. For being so old, the house was in pretty good shape, with just a few cracks in the plaster. Even the hardwood floors practically gleamed a golden hue. The high baseboard trim matched the color of the floor, complimenting the eggshell color of the walls. Someone had done a lot of work renovating and painting the house, since it had been built.

"What do you think?"

At Josh's voice she turned and saw him scoop Avril up into his arms, buzzing her neck with his chin, giving her a scratchy whisker burn, and grinning when the tot burst out in giggles.

She smiled, watching the beams of sunshine light up the colored glass in the transom above the door. But even more than the light airy feeling in the entranceway, it was the relaxed calm that showed in Josh that she found reassuring. From the glint in his blue eyes to the smile of pride looking around, it was obvious that he loved the house and the country setting. Maybe this would be a good move for the family. "It's lovely. Very impressive."

Paige wandered into the room where Amanda stood gazing out an expansive window into the side yard. An ancient maple tree extended thick gray branches over the lush lawn while its leaves showed the first hint of autumn with some yellows and orange foliage.

Her hand rose to muss Julian's hair and she bent to speak softly, in his ear. "That tree looks perfect for a tire swing, or even a tree house."

He turned to look at her with such an elated expression that she had to smile. Oh, to be that young again, that a tire swing could spark such happiness.

"Maybe when we get settled, your Dad could set that up for you." Paige winked and then rose to gaze out the window, past where the tree stood. "How close is the lake? I thought you said you were right next to it."

Amanda took a deep breath and grinned. "We are! It's just past that copse of trees, a five minute walk at most, you'll see. There's a flagstone path that leads to a dock and a small beach." Her eyes brightened. "The previous owners even left us an aluminum rowboat!" She spun in a circle with her arms outstretched. "There's seven acres of land. Isn't that amazing? Especially considering how small our lot in Toronto was." She pointed out a garden shed built next to the house. "That shed's almost the size of the back yard we had in the old place!"

"A garden shed? I thought this place came with a barn?"

Amanda nodded. "Yeah, it's down a path at the back of the house. I guess the owners put this here so they could keep the lawn mower handy in the summer and the snow blower in the winter." She shrugged. "Anyway, that's what Josh figures." She chuckled. "He *can't wait* to use a snow blower!" Shaking her head, she added, "Boys and their toys..."

"Hey! It's a tool, not a toy!" Josh said, still cuddling Avril.

"Whatever." Amanda grinned and gestured to her sister. "What's really crazy is that this place cost way less than our old house. It's bigger, on the water with land and a barn and we got it for a song! And the taxes on it are half of what we were paying in Toronto. Crazy huh?"

Josh rocked back and forth from his toes to his heels looking rather smug, while Avril's tiny fist closed over his nose, getting back at him for the buzzing.

Amanda turned from the window and pulling Paige along, she continued, "This is the dining room. Come on. The kitchen's just through here." Amanda was practically vibrating, leading the way through the archway into a mammoth sized kitchen, with a centre island and yards of countertop.

Paige's mouth fell open, gazing around the room, marveling at the banks of cabinets and the window that looked out to the back yard and the path to the barn. The renovations that she'd noticed in the entranceway were dwarfed by what was in this room. This was where the bulk of the money and time had been spent.

"There's room for a table but I think we'll put in a desk instead and use the island for meals. That way, I'll have a start on an office, setting up my business with boarding animals." Amanda stepped over to the side wall where there was a narrow door. She opened it and stepped back, "See this. A pantry! As if we'd need it with all these cabinets."

Paige could only stand and stare, totally gob smacked. The house, particularly the kitchen, was amazing! Why would anyone go to so much trouble to renovate the home and then leave it? And then to sell it for such a low price? Even taking into consideration that market value was lower in the smaller city, it seemed too good to be true.

A sharp crash followed by the sound of glass breaking made her jump!

Paige's heart was in her mouth as she looked around at the others...everyone was there except for... "Oh no! Julian!"

She turned and raced through the dining room and up the staircase, hearing Josh's footsteps right behind her.

She took the stairs two at a time, spinning around the newel post at the top to sprint down the hallway. "Julian?"

Behind her, Josh also called to his son.

She passed two empty rooms before spotting him sitting on the floor, his legs splayed wide. A blackbird, it's head twisted and facing backwards, lay next to him. She gasped seeing the long shards of glass scattered near Julian's leg.

The air felt heavy and hard to breathe as she scurried over to him and sank to her knees. She scooped him close, examining his face and arms for cuts.

The small boy pulled back and looked up at his father. "I didn't do it, Daddy. I came into the room and walked over to the window and then...then..." He started to cry and turned his face into Paige's shirt.

"Is Julian okay?" Amanda's voice rose from the stairwell, followed by the fast thuds of her feet in the hallway.

"He's fine." Josh called out before carefully nudging the glass away from his son's legs. "Why the hell would a bird fly into the window? There must have been something wrong with it to do that." He squatted down next to Paige and Julian, rubbing his son's back softly. "It's okay, buddy." He smiled wanly. "Wow. You're really not having a great day, Julian."

Paige's heart thudded hard in her chest and it wasn't just from the race up the stairs. Poor Julian could have been badly cut if the glass had hit him. And it had been close. Josh was right. Birds didn't just fly into windows hard enough to shatter them. She looked around and it hit her. This was the same room where she'd seen the glint of light flash.

She shuddered and held Julian tighter to her body.

# CHAPTER FIVE

A t Barney's barking in the front yard and the sound of a truck engine, Josh clamoured to his feet and peeked out the window. "It's the movers. Can you guys go down and let them in? I'll clean this mess up."

Paige saw a crimson pool of blood spreading near the dead bird's beak, the eye above dull and glazed. Her stomach rolled and she swallowed the bile that rose in the back of her throat. It was sickening seeing the dead bird. But the sight of the glass was more disturbing, so close to slicing Julian's legs. The poor kid had only been looking out the window when the bird dive bombed through it.

She took his hand and led him from the room, following Amanda and Avril down the stairs. A burly man, the driver of the moving truck by the looks of his blue work shirt, stood in the open doorway, petting the dog's head. He looked up and smiled, "Quite a watch dog you've got here. A Bouvier des Flandres, right?"

Barney licked his hand, and turned big brown eyes up, recognizing a dog lover. The second mover, a young, red-haired man with lean sinewy muscles showing below the sleeve of his T shirt stepped up onto the veranda. Barney turned, the hackles rising on the back of his thick neck, emitting a low growl.

The first guy, laughed and reached to rub Barney's head again. "He's also got good taste."

"Very funny." The younger man scowled and then flashed a slippery smile looking over at Amanda. "Can you show us where you want things to go?"

Amanda looked confused just for a moment, her gaze darting over to Paige. "Well...sure."

Paige stepped over to her sister and reached for Avril. "I'll take the kids outside and we'll explore with Barney. We'll just be in the way here." She stepped past the first mover and signaled with a jerk of her head for Julian to follow. "C'mon Barney. You too." The dog immediately began to pad after her.

The second mover gave her the once-over with his eyes, not bothering to even pretend that he wasn't. Her eyes narrowed and she held her head high, purposely ignoring him. The creep. No wonder Barney had growled at him.

It was funny. She was used to guys sizing her up and even the odd wolf whistle but there were some guys that could make you want to take a shower with just a not so subtle glance. Moving guy number two was one of those types.

Julian skipped ahead of her, running to the side of the house where the big maple tree was. "C'mon, Aunt Paige!"

His excitement, the soles of his feet flying high was enough for Avril to want to join him.

"Down." Avril squirmed and Paige was forced to set her down quickly or risk the child slipping out of her grasp. She ran after her bigger brother. "Julie! Wait for me!"

Paige had to suppress a smile watching the boy turn and shoot his little sister an evil look. No matter how many times he corrected Avril, she still called him Julie. Maybe because she knew it bugged him? Paige remembered doing something similar to that with Amanda when she was younger, emphasizing the 'man' part of her name.

Julian clung to the rough bark of the tree, trying to get a toe hold to climb it. His fingers clawed into it, but his sneakers kept slipping. Avril stood silently watching him, her thumb in her mouth.

Paige stepped closer and scooped him up, holding him high in the air under the lowest branch. "Grab hold of the branch, Julian." She stretched higher and felt his weight lighten in her hands as he grasped it. She pulled her hands back, hovering close to his body, ready to catch him again.

"Hey! Look at me!" Julian kicked his feet back and forth, swinging from the branch.

Avril tugged at Paige's shirt. "Now me. My turn."

Just at that moment, Julian's grip slipped and she caught him, easing the fall down to the leaf littered ground. He brushed his hands together and laughed while Paige turned to Avril. "Sorry hon, another year or so and you can try too."

Julian was off again, disappearing around the back of the house. Paige scooped Avril up and stepped quickly after him. Uh oh. Until she knew the lay of the land here, she needed to keep an eye on him.

At the back of the house, near the back door was a flagstone patio, half covered by a grape arbor. Julian ran by it, and headed down the path on his way to a squat building topped with an upper cupola.

Paige's brow became tight and with Avril in tow, she hurried to catch up to him. Barney snuffling along, took up the rear.

Coming up the path, Paige came to the dark wooden structure. "Is *this* the barn?" she asked.

"Yeah," said Julian. "It looks weird."

"Looks more like a small church." The only barns Paige had ever been in were large airy buildings, walls that stood two stories high topped with a roof that gently arched like a half moon. The structure before her had low walls that supported a sharply peaked roof. It was more like a two-car garage and the roof resembled the one at St. Magdalene's Church. She craned her neck upward. How in the world could you shingle that thing? It rose up to a point that was at least forty feet above the ground. She shook her head in puzzlement.

The two doors at the front were much smaller than typical barn doors, not much bigger than a set of double doors in a nice home. A high-pitched squeal pierced through her when one of the doors inched open.

Her eyes flashed wide and her heart leapt to her throat watching Julian creep closer to the building. Ger gaze shifted to the slice of darkness between the doors, and she gasped. "Julian! Wait!"

Mirroring her fear, the dog bounded past her and stopped short, barking at the dark opening.

Julian came to a complete halt, stopping so fast his body almost toppled over onto the packed earth in front of him. His arms shot out to the side, trying to keep his balance and grab onto the bristling dog beside him.

When Paige reached him, his dark eyes spanned wide in a face that had gone suddenly pale. Barney's lips pulled back, snarling and a low growl rumbled in his throat.

The high-pitched cry of the rusty hinges still protested as the door continued slowly opening. The hair on Paige's arms tingled as she stood stock still, watching.

Then, as quick as a bolt of lightning it banged shut with a force than she reverberated in her gut. Oh my God! Her heart pounded fast and she hugged Avril in closer.

Barney's hackles were high, his barks thundering in the air. She felt Julian sidle close to her thigh, his hand clutching her jeans. Avril too, hearing the loud bang, and the dog's angry noise, snuggled her head into Paige's neck, sucking her thumb with a furious intensity.

Oh God. She had to be strong. She took a deep breath and then her hand rubbed Julian's shoulder, turning both of them around to walk back. "Shush Barney! C'mon boy." Her mind was going a mile a minute. "That must have been some breeze, causing that door to slam like that, huh? There must be a window open in there. We'll just wait until your Mommy and Daddy are with us before we explore the barn. What do you think?"

She continued striding to the patio next to the back door, the dog at her side still rumbling a few growls.

Even to her own ears, the explanation sounded phony. There wasn't any breeze. The day was sunny and calm with only a few clouds in the sky.

Her head tilted to the side as another thought flashed in her brain. This was the country, not the city. Shouldn't there be crickets or birds calling? She looked around, feeling the brightness of the day burn her eyes, the intensity of the grass and the blue sky suddenly unnaturally bright. There was a palpable sense of quiet, a thick, other-worldly atmosphere.

She tried the back door and her jaw tightened finding it locked. Gripping Julian's hand, together the three of them rounded the building. The moving men near the front steps, hoisted the refrigerator up a metal ramp to the front door. The older, dark-haired guy laughed, seemingly still teasing the younger one, who rolled his eyes.

In the doorway, Amanda and Josh stood chatting waiting for the guys to come across the veranda.

Despite the normalcy of the scene, she paused. Her vision became wavy and she faltered to the side trying to overcome the sudden dizziness.

When Julian raced up the stairs to his parents, Paige gulped a deep breath, her mind grasping at anything to make sense of what had happened.

That door banging shut in the barn...it probably *was* just the breeze. There had to be some logical explanation for it. She'd probably see the cause when Josh and Amanda showed them the rest of the property.

But why had all of them been so scared? Even the dog had sensed something ominous.

# CHAPTER SIX

Amanda left the veranda and walked around the jeep to its back door. She turned to Paige and the kids and smiled. "Anyone hungry? Help me with this cooler will you, Paige?"

Paige walked over to Amanda and set Avril down. Seeing the cooler reminded her that she hadn't eaten anything since early that morning. It was probably why she'd felt a little woozy a few moments before. The dead bird and then the slamming barn door hadn't helped her nerves either.

Amanda handed a blanket to her son. "Take this around to the big maple tree, Julian. Our first meal in the new house is going to be a picnic. How does that sound?"

His eyes lit up and he raced off to the big tree, Barney and Avril trailing behind.

Amanda grabbed the handle of the bulky red cooler and helped Paige hoist it out of the jeep's hatch. "Wow. This is hard work. Remind me never to buy another house. This is my last move."

Paige laughed and looked over at her sister. "Hopefully, you're right, this will be the last time. Seriously, what more could you want in a house? And on a lake? Awesome. Although I confess, I'm not crazy about the barn."

A 'V' formed between Amanda's eyebrows when she looked over at Paige. "Why? It's a nice size and it's in really good shape."

'Let it go,' she thought to herself. Shrugging, she said, "Just not my style, I guess."

Amanda shrugged but her mouth pulled to the side, a teeny bit miffed. "Oh well, it is what it is."

They were almost at the tree, where Julian tugged at the edges of the blanket, trying to spread it out, despite Avril and Barney's 'help'. Paige glanced over at her sister. It probably wouldn't be a good idea to talk about the barn right then. With the kids there, it'd be better to downplay it.

She set her side of the cooler down and plopped down next to Avril. The little girl flashed a wide grin before turning to wait for Amanda and lunch.

Amanda opened the cooler and set a plastic container of sandwiches in the centre of the blanket, and then scooped up the juice boxes. Paige popped the lid and handed a peanut butter and jelly to Avril.

Paige looked over at Amanda, watching as she plucked a rubber disc from the cooler and popped it, creating a small bowl which she then filled with water for the dog. One thing about her sister...when she was well and on her game she could be super organized. She'd even considered Barney's needs at the picnic.

Julian munched on his sandwich and swallowed hard, looking excitedly at his mother. "This tree is pretty awesome. Think Daddy will have time today to put up a tire swing for me?"

Paige had to laugh at the look that Amanda shot her. She turned to Julian and smiled. "If we can find a tire and rope, I probably can help you with that. At least something temporary until your dad can get it set up."

Amanda nodded. "That's a good idea. It'll give you something to do while we get the house sorted out. I think you might find some rope in the barn. Not sure about a tire though." She unpacked another sandwich and bit into her lunch.

The smile on Paige's lips froze. The thought of going into the barn made her stomach sink lower. But Julian was hopped up about the swing and she *had* given him the idea...

"Hey Amanda?" Josh ambled across the grass and plopped down next to them. "When you're done lunch, can you go in and let the movers know where to put the bedroom furniture? They've got the kitchen appliances in and the living room's almost done. They're going to need you to sort through the bedroom stuff." He flopped down on the blanket.

"Daddy? Will you help Aunt Paige set up a tire swing for me and Avril?" Julian edged forward and looked up into his father's blue eyes, an older version of his own. "Please?"

Paige let out a small sigh of relief. At least there'd be another adult with her going to get the rope. "C'mon Josh." She rose to her feet. "Help me look in the barn. I can get this set up while you and Amanda work with the movers."

"No rest for the wicked." He looked up at her and once more rose to his feet.

When Julian started to get up, Paige's hand rose up like a traffic cop. "No. You stay here buddy. It'll be faster if you just let your Dad and me look. Besides which, your Mom hasn't seen you too much today. Stay and finish your lunch with her and Avril."

"No, it's fine, hon," Amanda said. "Avril and I can have some girl time!" She gave the toddler a tickle.

Josh fell into step beside her walking around the house to the back, and Julian was on her other side. Three abreast, they went down the path to the barn. The doors were once more agape, swaying and creaking a little. The cold tightness in the back of her neck was only lessened a little with Josh walking next to her, going into the creepy old building together.

She risked a peek up at Josh. Did he find the back yard strange? What was with the deathly quiet back there? Not a bird or even a cricket chirping. She took a deep breath and squared her shoulders. "The barn door banged shut when the kids and I were here earlier. It scared the hell out of us."

"Hmm. I wonder if some animal got in there. A raccoon or something. But, the doors should have been latched." His face tightened into a grimace and he shook his head. "Let me go in first. I know where the light switch is and if some critter is inside..." With a sigh, he took a tentative step to the opening, peeking inside.

Paige crept slowly after him, trying to pierce the darkness with her eyes. The hair on her arms tingled and she held her breath looking past her brother-in-law. There was the strangest sense that they weren't alone in there. It was as if someone was watching them. She gripped Julian's hand tightly. Two steps in, she stopped. The only sound was her heartbeat doing double time.

Light flashed from a bare bulb hanging a few feet from the door. Josh turned around and his smile was fleeting before scanning the room looking for whatever had caused the door to shut.

At Barney's thundering bark Paige almost jumped out of her skin! "Shit! Shut up, Barney!"

At the flash of movement, she and Julian jumped back letting out a high yelp. The white tipped tail of a deer, disappeared with a flash of dark hooves out the opening of the barn. Barney raced after it, barking with a frenzy.

"Barney! Come!" Josh hurried past her, gripping the side of the door, and peering after the dog.

In a moment, the dog once more appeared, its tongue lolling while its dark eyes shone with excitement, so pleased with himself.

"Good boy." Josh chuckled and rubbed the dog behind its ear before turning to her. "I guess that solves the mystery of the doors banging shut. It must have bumped against them earlier. Strange though...I never would have thought a deer would go *into* a barn. Maybe because it's been vacant for a while? I don't know."

Paige's hand still covered her chest, trying to still her racing heart. She took a deep breath and blew it out slowly, letting out a laugh as well. "Wow. Never would have expected to meet *Bambi* in here."

Josh clicked the latch and held the two doors closed for a moment examining them. "I think I need to tighten some screws here. The latch isn't quite catching." He huffed a sigh. "Let me grab my tool box. I'll be right back."

Paige and Julian looked at each other while they waited.

She tilted her head at him. "You want to go back inside?"

The five-year-old looked at her with steady eyes. "No. Let's wait for Dad, okay?"

Yeah, this place creeped him out too.

Josh was back quickly, carrying his tool box. He looked over at both of them, then squatted down with his tool box and took out a screwdriver. As he tightened the screws on the latch, he said, "Why don't you two look for some rope?" Stepping inside for a moment, He flicked on the light switch again. "Go ahead."

The barn was an empty space with a dirt floor. At the back of the barn was a long work table that was about chest-high. There was a shelf below, holding odds and ends in a jumbled mess, but no sign of a rope.

As they walked up the center of the barn floor a wave of nausea rolled through her when she was about halfway across. What the hell? She looked over to Julian. He was a picture of terror with mouth gaping and the whites of his eyes showing.

"You okay?" she asked, making an effort to swallow the bitter bile at the back of her mouth.

"I don't think so. Something's bad in here." His nose wrinkled. "I feel sick, like I'm going to throw up."

Paige sniffed the air. "Yeah, me too. But I don't smell anything."

She looked to the back of the open area where a ladder stretched upwards. She peered harder, but she couldn't make out a hayloft. Following the line of the ladder as it disappeared up into the darkness made her suddenly feel dizzy. She'd have to tell Josh to take that damn thing down. If one of the kids climbed up it, they could break their necks.

She looked up at the high roof, the narrow glints of sunlight coming in through cracks between the dark boards. Her hand rose and she scooped her hair to the side, holding it in her hand. There could be bats up there in the rafters. For sure there was a whole host of spiders from the number of webs floating in sheets everywhere. Yuck.

Finished with the latch, Josh came inside. Julian followed him to the back area, where he rooted around, looking for a rope.

"Well, looky here," said Josh, peering under the long table that had been built along one side. His hand reached in and pulled out a rusted horse shoe.

"What's that?" Julian smiled and stared up at his father.

"It's a horse shoe, son."

"What's it for?"

"It's for horses. They put them on the bottom of their feet so they won't wear out their hooves." He held the rusted piece of curved steel out and the boy took it.

Julian ducked his head under the table. "Shouldn't there be more? I mean, horses have four feet, right?"

Josh nodded. "Yeah, they do." He took the horseshoe back and hefted it. "I think this was for another purpose though."

"Like what?"

"As a good luck charm." Josh rummaged in his tool box and came up with a couple of nails and his hammer. He walked over to the doors of the barn. It was an easy reach when he centered the horseshoe over the doors, and with the ends pointing up, nailing it loosely to the frame. When he was done, he tugged at it so it rattled a little.

"Don't you need to nail some more, Dad?" Julian asked.

"Nope. Some old guy once told me to make sure that the shoe was a little loose. That way it can pick up more good luck."

"Good luck?"

"Yeah. That's what a horseshoe is. You put it over the door with the ends pointing up for good luck."

"I thought you said they were for horses."

Josh laughed. "Yeah, I did, didn't I?" He tapped the talisman over the door. "They're also a good luck charm."

Paige stood silently watching the entire exchange and smirked. "Good luck with it not falling off and hitting you in the head." She giggled. "That would be a real kick in the head. Kick... horse shoe... get it?"

"Don't give up the day job, smart ass. Comedy's not your forte." He looked back to the table. "Let's see if there's any rope over on that side." He walked to the other side of the table and lifted an old milk crate. "Found some!" Josh tossed a coil of thick grey rope her way.

Stepping away from the table, he opened a normal sized door at the back of the barn, letting in a beam of natural light. "I think I saw a tire out here," he said as he walked out the door, leaving it open.

She held the rope at her side and took a deep breath, inhaling the ancient smell of hay, and animals in the dust motes filtering through the air. The room was warm and sickeningly sweet. It needed a good airing out at the very least, although even then it would never be a place where she'd want to hang out. No. There was definitely something creepy about the barn. Josh acted like he didn't notice anything, but she felt it in her gut.

He appeared once more, grinning and wheeling a truck tire in front of him. "I knew I'd seen one of these when we looked at the place." He continued on, grinning at her as he walked by and out the huge front doors.

"Yay, Dad!" Julian raced after his father leaving Paige behind.

She shuddered, feeling a blast of cool air flit by her neck. She looked around and then sprinted after them out into the bright, clean air.

# CHAPTER SEVEN

Barney sat patiently near the house, watching Josh and Julian when she stepped outside. He rose to his feet and gave a few excited yips, running to join them. When they rounded the corner of the house and Amanda with Avril in her arms came into view, Julian raced ahead.

"Look Mommy! We found one. A tire swing!"

Paige smiled watching Josh trying to keep the tire upright and rolling. When he got to the blanket, he let the tire fall to its side and he put his arm around Amanda's waist. Julian snuggled into his leg on one side, while Avril was on the other, grinning and reaching for the tire. Even Barney sat down on the corner of the blanket, his adoring gaze at his family palpable. It was a sight straight out of a Norman Rockwell painting.

Amanda gave Avril's waist a quick tickle and dodged the tot's pudgy arms before turning to Paige. "You've got your work cut out for you, Sis, getting that tire swing up!" She clapped Paige on the shoulder and then turned to Josh. "I'd better get back in there before they put the furniture in the wrong rooms."

Josh gave the tire a final push towards Paige, catching her in the thigh. He flopped down onto the blanket and reached for the cooler. "You sure you can manage this?" He grinned at her and then bit into his sandwich.

She steadied the tire with her fingertips and swung the loop of rope in her other hand. "We're going to soon find out, aren't we?"

Julian stepped over and pulled the tire from her hand, trying to roll it over the grass on his own. His sister followed, pouncing on the tire when it tilted and fell to the side.

Paige looked up at a branch that was just high enough to give a good swing to the tire when it was mounted. She tossed the loop of rope up, and shook her head when it brushed the smooth bark of the branch and fell to the ground.

"Step back and toss it like you're throwing a basketball, trying to edge by the hoop." Josh leaned back, propping his upper body up with his arm, his legs casually spread on the cotton blanket. "Come on Paige. Didn't you used to be the basketball star in high school? You can do it."

She coiled the end of the thick rope over her wrist and then bunched it, stepping back and tossing it high onto the branch. When it slipped over and fell to the ground on the other side, she grinned. It was about five feet over her head and she'd managed. She still had the touch.

Josh finished his sandwich and sprang to his feet. He grabbed the end of the rope and tied a knot, leaving a six-inch loop. "We'll just thread the end through and..." He tugged the rope, grinning as the slip knot rose higher, ending under the branch. "There. You should be able to manage the tire." He smiled and then walked across the grass to join Amanda inside.

Paige sat down on the blanket and dug around in the cooler for another sandwich and soft drink.

"Higher!" Avril clung to the sides of the tire swing while Julian gently pushed her back and forth.

Paige fished her cell phone from her shirt pocket and snapped a photo of them. The sun's rays flitting through the maple's leaves cast a dappled pattern on the grass surrounding them, while the high pitched whirr of cicadas broke the late summer stillness.

"My turn." Julian stopped the tire's pendulum-like swing and Avril slipped off the rim, edging her feet down onto the grass.

The little tyke's thumb rose and immediately popped into her mouth and she trudged slowly over to flop down next to Paige, putting her head in her aunt's lap. It had been an exciting day for the little girl and she was ready for her nap.

"Can you push me?" Julian's feet just about reached the ground but not quite.

"Sorry buddy. You'll have to push off with your feet and manage on your own." Paige shrugged and her fingers gently brushed Avril's fine mane of hair. The child was already drifting off to sleep.

She smiled watching Avril's mouth grow still and the thumb fall from between her lips. She was an angel sleeping peacefully, so snug and secure next to her aunt. Julian swung steadily back and forth, pleased with his independence making the tire move. Even Barney was flaked out in the shade, his ear twitching at the odd fly that happened by.

She heard the engine of the moving truck start up and then it came into view, driving along the narrow road beside the farm. Well, that was that. Their stuff was here and this was their new home.

# CHAPTER EIGHT

At the touch on her shoulder, Paige woke with a start. Amanda squatted down on the blanket next to her and pried Avril's sleeping body up from her lap.

"Here, Aunt Paige." Julian handed the cell phone back to her. "Guess what? I got to level four in Jungle Run."

Paige smiled at him and took a deep breath before rising to her feet and stretching. The sun was a little lower in the sky when she looked around. She must have dozed off along with Avril.

"We've got the beds in the kids' rooms set up. I made your bed but I left the other stuff for you to arrange." Amanda glanced over as she walked beside her. Julian had skipped ahead, running beside the dog.

"Thanks Amanda." Paige gave her sister a one-armed hug and smiled. She hesitated for a moment and looked back at the cooler and picnic items.

"Don't worry about that. Josh will get it later. You never got to see everything upstairs before the movers showed up and..." Amanda's eyes flashed to Julian who was just rounding the side of the house. "I taped cardboard over the broken window to keep the bugs out. Hopefully we can get it repaired this week." She pulled a face, edging to the side when she spoke, "I hope you don't mind but that's the room where we put your things. It's the next biggest after the master bedroom."

Paige's stomach tightened but she managed a smile looking over at her sister. "No. No problem. I don't think Julian would care for that room anyway, not after the bird flying in. The thing's gone, right?"

"Oh yeah. Josh took care of it."

They came around to the front of the house in time to see Julian race up the few veranda steps and disappear through the open door into the house. Paige looked up at the second story window which the bird had broken. A dark brown square perched above the lower half of the window. She sighed, looking past it to the upper half. Well, at least the rest of the window was intact and she'd be able to see out. Still, the sight of the blackbird with its broken neck, the small pool of blood, flashed in her mind, sending a shiver through her shoulders.

When they walked in the door, Josh glanced over and gripping his cell phone tight, strode into the other room on the right. Paige glanced over at Amanda but from the shrug of her sister's shoulders, she was also in the dark about the phone call. Just the odd snippet of Josh's voice was distinguishable—something about asphalt and oil?

Paige sighed. Work. Oh, for Heaven's sake! It was his moving day and they couldn't get someone else to deal with whatever had come up?

Amanda's eyebrows rose and she also sighed, before leading the way up the wide staircase. She turned to the right at the top and carried the still sleeping Avril into one of the bedrooms. Paige spotted the low pink bed with the side rail at the far wall of the room where Amanda gently laid the small child. Avril rolled onto her side, plunked her thumb back into her mouth, and was right back asleep.

Down the hall on the other side, the steady, dull thump from the room at the front of the house drew Paige's attention. She tiptoed over the golden hardwood floor and peeked in, only to find Julian grinning and bouncing high on his bed, completely bunching up the red race car themed spread.

He was lost in his own world, enjoying his room so she left him there, creeping softly across the hall to the room where the bird had entered earlier—her room.

Avoiding the window, she gazed at the rest of it and smiled. Even with her queen-sized bed, there was still lots of space for the dresser and desk. And the wall color, a creamy eggshell complimented the muted plaid of her duvet. The last rays of the sun shone through the half window onto the stack of boxes set next to the curved chaise lounge. She smiled. This would be fine and it wasn't like she'd be there forever, only until she was sure her sister was settled and doing well.

Amanda appeared in the doorway, a tentative, half smile on her lips. "How do you like it? Hope you don't mind sharing the bathroom with the kids. Josh and I have our own bath adjoining the master bedroom."

Paige laughed and began opening the suitcase set on the bed. "Sharing a bathroom? I can think of worse things than finding a rubber ducky hiding behind the shower curtain." More than once in the past year she'd shared the kids' bathroom. The only thing new this time was that Amanda was well enough to notice and care about the slight inconvenience.

At the sound of Josh's footsteps coming down the hallway, Paige looked over at the doorway.

His hands rested on Amanda's shoulders and he gazed down into her eyes. "Sorry babe. I'm not going to be able to take next week off, after all. It's crazy busy and they need me in Montreal ASAP for a meeting." He turned and for a few moments his eyes locked with Paige's.

Her neck muscles tightened and she nodded slightly. It would be okay. Even though she'd counted on him being around for a little while longer getting settled, eventually she was going to have to get used to it, being on her own keeping an eye on things. It had to be important at work for him to cut the time with the kids and Amanda so short.

Amanda sighed but seeing the anxious look on Josh's face, she took a deep breath and her chin rose high. "We've still got the weekend with you and we'll get most of the unpacking done." She took his hand and looked over at Paige. "How about we give you some time alone to finish in here? I really appreciate you keeping the kids busy earlier. Thanks Paige."

She watched the two of them leave and heard their voices fade as they wandered down the hall. Josh leaving early was just a minor hiccup. She lifted a couple of dresses from the suitcase and walked over to the closet to begin hanging things up.

When she opened the closet door, she noticed a small wooden box tucked at the far side, on the floor. After hanging the clothes, she bent and picked the box up. The varnish was old and chipped, but inlaid swirls of different types of wood still showed on the lid above a brass latch. Her fingers tingled when she pinched the old-fashioned wind-up key protruding from the back of the box.

She eyed the small antique as she drifted across the room and sank down on the bed. Her fingernail hooked in the latch, opening it and she lifted the lid. A whiff of something sweet, like camphor drifted from the red velvet lining inside. A brass cylinder, punctuated with Braille-like tiny dots, was mounted next to a fine-metal tooth comb. A music box? She twisted the key at the back, winding the small mechanism until it became tight.

When she let go of the key, hollow, bell-like sounds rose in the air. Her mouth fell open as she listened to the music. The tune was melancholy, something that bespoke of bygone days, filled with a wistful longing. The tines of the comb lifted and each time one was displaced by a blip in the brass cylinder, ringing a tinny, hollow note.

Her chin drooped lower, almost to her chest as she gazed down at the rolling brass tube. The tension of the day melted and her shoulders sagged lower. There was nothing but the tinkling tune of the box resting softly in her warm and heavy hands. Her breath slowed and she drifted into the faint melody.

"Aunt Paige?"

She jerked upright. Her fingers became claws clutching the box when Julian's voice broke the reverie. Couldn't they just leave her alone for one minute? It had been so peaceful resting quietly, caught up in the soft music.

Her eyes narrowed looking over at the small boy, his hands holding the toy truck. "What do you want now?"

His mouth fell open while he stared blankly at her for a moment. He couldn't even make eye contact, gazing past her shoulder. With a start, he spun on his heels and ran down the hallway, his high-pitched voice calling for his mother.

For a few seconds, a blank numbness filled Paige's body. Her throat began to thicken and she swallowed the lump forming there. Oh no. She'd never spoken so sharply to him before...scaring him so bad that he'd run away from her!

She snapped the lid of the music box shut and scampered to her feet. If she hadn't been so caught up in the haunting beauty of the box and the tune, she wouldn't have snapped at her nephew. What was wrong with her?

Still...She looked down at the box. It was a beautiful antique. If she had to venture a guess, she'd wager it was probably over a hundred years old. It had to be worth a fair bit of money. Why would anyone leave it behind? Again, the tips of her fingers tingled as she stood deliberating what to do with it. She couldn't just leave it out on her dresser and risk the kids breaking it.

She walked to the closet and set the box back where she'd found it. When it left her hand, she knew that it wasn't just fear of Julian breaking it that made her want to hide it away again. This was something she'd discovered in her room. It was hers...at least until she figured out what to do with it. It had been nice holding it, listening to the old-fashioned melody.

After a brisk brush of her hands together, the dust scattering off, she continued unpacking the rest of her clothes. The suitcase slid softly on the wooden floor and was soon out of sight under her bed. In no time flat she had gone through the boxes sitting beside her chaise lounge. She hummed the tune she'd heard and with her arms full of toiletries, she strode down the hall to the bathroom she would share with the kids.

———⋈———

In Paige's bedroom, the white eyelet lace dress she'd hung carefully in the closet slipped from the hanger. It ended up a pile over the music box, shrouding it. Three muffled tinny notes sounded, then stopped.

# Chapter Nine

*The next day...*

Paige's eye creaked open at the soft pat on her arm. Avril stood next to the bed watching her with doe-eyed innocence, the ragged, one eyed bunny tucked in the crook of her arm. It was early morning but not so early that the sun hadn't made an appearance. She yawned and threw the duvet off to the side. The kids getting her up at the crack of dawn was the down side to living at Amanda's. Left to her own devices, she would sleep until noon.

The smile that teased the corners of Avril's lips, her eyes becoming brighter made it all worthwhile though. Paige pushed herself up and out of the bed. "Hey Avril. Ready to get dressed?"

Avril nodded. Her tiny bare feet raced across the room and she disappeared down the hallway.

Paige grabbed her light cotton robe from the chaise lounge where she'd laid it out the night before. As she slipped it over her shoulders, she blinked wide a few times to clear the sleepiness. Surprisingly, she'd slept well, especially considering it was a new place. It was such a change from the big city, so quiet, no ambulance or police sirens or big trucks screaming by.

When she stepped inside Avril's room the little girl hugged the bunny tight, staring at something across the room. Paige glanced over but the only thing breaking the monotony of the beige wall was the closet door gaping open. Avril giggled and then turned to face Paige, dropping the bunny and pushing down on the waistband of her pajamas.

"Hold on there, Avril. Let me get a change pad and some clothes first." Paige snatched the lined pad from the change table and spread it on the floor. She hated using the high table now that Avril was so big. It probably wouldn't be much longer that the toddler would need a diaper at night. She was practically perfect during the day, using the potty.

She leaned over and opened the drawer in the table, rooting around for undies and an outfit for the day. All the while, Avril stood in front of Paige, her tiny hands resting on her aunt's thighs while she peeked around at something behind them.

"Here we go!" Paige held up the blue jean shorts and a pink top, smiling down at Avril. But the little tyke was intent on whatever game she was playing, peeking around and ducking back with a shrieking giggle.

Paige dropped the clothes onto the floor and she tickled Avril's neck and shoulders. She began singing one of Avril's favorites, "We're gonna shake, shake, shake the sillies out."

Scooping Avril's legs out from under her, she lowered her niece onto the change mat. "Someone's in a silly mood today." In a flash the toddler's diaper and pajamas lay in a heap and she was dressed in shorts and a T shirt.

When she took the little girl's hand and led the way from the room, Amanda was just emerging from her bedroom. "How'd you sleep last night?" She flashed a smile at Paige and then bent to pick Avril up, giving her cheek a kiss.

There was a warmth in her chest when Paige looked at Amanda, seeing her already up and dressed for the day, looking after Avril now. This was definitely a good sign. "Great, actually; I slept like a rock. It's so quiet here." Paige stepped across the hall and hesitated, about to go into the bathroom. "How about you?"

"Wonderful. Of course we were pretty tired from the move but even so, I like the peace and quiet." Amanda took a step down the stairs and then turned to Paige again. "I'm afraid it'll be just pastries for breakfast. I'm going grocery shopping today to stock up."

Paige nodded. "Need some help with that?"

"No. I'm good. Josh mentioned taking the kids swimming at the lake, Maybe you could join them. After working so hard yesterday, you need a break. It'll be fun."

Julian and Barney raced down the hallway, scampering between Paige and Amanda. "We're going swimming?" The young boy grinned up at his mother.

She ruffled his hair and bent to kiss his cheek. "Yeah. Hey! How about saying good morning to your Aunt Paige?"

Paige looked down for a moment picturing the hurt look in his eyes when she'd spoken sharply to him the day before.

There was just a momentary hesitation before he spoke, his eyes searching hers. "Hi Aunt Paige. Are you coming swimming too?"

"You bet!" A slow smile spread on her cheeks and she let out a long breath. It was like the music box thing the day before hadn't happened.

"Come on, Julian. Give your aunt a chance to get ready for the day. Your dad's fixing breakfast."

Paige turned and went into the bathroom, closing the door softly behind her. She would make it up to Julian later that day. And she hadn't been swimming in a lake since she was a kid camping with her family. This would be fun.

Twenty minutes later, finished in the bathroom, she wandered back to her own room to get dressed. She slipped the bathing suit on and then stepped over to the closet to get the terry-cloth cover-up. The white lace dress laying in a heap on the floor caught her eye. She could have sworn she'd hung it up so that the shoulder straps hooked into the hanger's slots.

She picked up the dress, and her fingers brushed the satiny wood of the music box. For an instant the skin on the back of her neck prickled and she felt an icy chill wash over her bare arm. She looked down at the box and jumped when a single note sounded, high and ringing hollow.

Her heart was in her throat and she jerked her hand away quickly. Staring at the box, she took a deep breath. She must have jostled it making the roller move.

She hooked the dress onto the hanger, purposely threading the spaghetti straps inside the thin slotted hooks to ensure it stayed put. When she placed the hanger on the rod, she glanced down once more at the music box.

There was something about it...she wanted to pick it up and listen to the tune again. It wasn't anything familiar, but rather some old tune that was kind of off-key and monotonous.

She sighed and bent to pick it up, standing in the closet opening and lifting the lid of the box slowly. Once more she twisted the wind-up key until it grew taut. The brass cylinder rolled slowly and the hollow bells of the tune filled her ears.

Paige's chin dropped and her vision blurred, listening to the melody. She sank down onto the floor, holding the box on her lap.

Her mind filled with the picture of a young girl in a full dress, twirling gracefully, her fingers pinching the hem on one side, holding it at waist height. White lace frothed under a shimmering forest green skirt and a flash of smooth tawny thigh flashed as she danced. Auburn hair swept her shoulders, the waves and curls red-hued when they caught the light.

The song stopped and Paige's eyes once more became focused. She blinked and shook her head slightly, seeing her own dresses hanging limp in the closet. She got to her feet, shaking her head at the sudden lapse into sitting around daydreaming, listening to an antique music box. She should be getting ready. Josh and the kids would wonder what was keeping her.

She set the box back down in the corner of the closet and spied her cover-up. She slipped it over her head and tightened the drawstring belt. At the sound of a car engine starting, she stepped over to the window and peeked down into the driveway. The black jeep was backing up and then turning to drive out the driveway. Amanda hadn't even waited until she was down for breakfast? The stores were probably not even open yet.

Paige slipped her feet into her sandals and left the bedroom. When she reached the bottom stair, Josh's voice coming from the living room caught her up short. She stepped in and saw Julian sprawled on the sofa playing a game on his small tablet while Avril colored a poster on the floor. Josh was in the midst of stacking a bookshelf, emptying a cardboard box at his feet.

"Hi Paige. I saved a pastry for you. There's still coffee in the pot if you want any but you may have to nuke it first." Josh finished the last few books in the box and picked the container up, already on his way over to the entrance. "We figure you went back to bed so we didn't bother you."

"What?"

Julian set the tablet aside and rose from the sofa. "Can we go now?" From the whiney way he asked, his patience had worn thin.

Paige's mouth fell open seeing the bottom of the kids' bathing suits peeking out from under the long T shirts. Even Josh was in his light clam-digger trunks, picking the stack of towels up that were set at the end of the sofa.

Avril got up and trudged over to Paige, lifting her arms to be picked up. Her thumb plopped into her mouth, a sure sign that she was ready for a nap. Her head snuggled under Paige's chin and the steady sound of her sucking her thumb drifted into Paige's ears.

Paige slid her cell phone out of her pocket and glanced at the time. She gasped seeing that it was now after nine o'clock. Oh my God. When she left her bedroom to get Avril changed it had been seven. Two hours had gone by since then. Two hours during which time she'd only managed to shower and get dressed.

She hugged Avril tighter to her body, and took a few deep breaths, fighting the sudden dizzy feeling that came over her. "I think I'll skip breakfast."

Josh turned and looked at his daughter. "She'll be okay until we get back. We won't be all that long and she can have a nap later. Maybe Amanda will be home by then."

When Julian skipped by, Barney the burly black dog raised its head from its forepaws, and got up from the mat by the front door.

Paige fell into step behind the troupe, heading through the dining room and out the kitchen door to the backyard. When she looked at the sky, the sun was almost directly overhead, and not a breath of breeze stirred the sultry air. A trickle of sweat rolled down the side of her face and she swept it away with her finger.

It was a perfect day to cool off in the lake. Her gut was tight watching Julian and Josh walk ahead of her on the flagstone path leading to the lake. The poor little tyke had waited so long for her to come down. And the time lapse... She'd never lost a chunk of time like that.

Ever.

# CHAPTER TEN

## *Later that day...*

As they trucked up the path refreshed from their swim, Josh paused and looked over at the barn doors. They gaped open once more.

"I have to fix those doors. I don't want to leave tomorrow and have another animal get in there for you guys to deal with." He sighed and walked over to the barn, leaving Paige with the two kids.

Julian was about to follow his father but Paige placed her hand on his shoulder, stopping him. "You'd better get out of that wet suit, kiddo. Besides, your mom might be home from the grocery store. Aren't you hungry for a popsicle?" It was a low blow, hitting him in the sweet tooth but she didn't feel right about him being in the barn. Josh could take care of himself and he'd be too busy working to pay much attention to his son.

"Okay. But what about Daddy? He's still in his wet bathing suit too?" He looked up at her, squinting when the sun peeked out from behind a fluffy white cloud.

"He'll be fine." Paige shifted Avril higher on her hip, adjusting the small child's weight in her tired arms. From the way she was sucking her thumb, she'd be out cold pretty soon.

Julian patted Barney's head and then skipped along the path, bumping into the dog's muscular back the odd time. When he reached the back door, it opened and Amanda stood there, holding an orange freezie out to her son. "I saw you coming," she said with a smile.

When Paige stepped closer, Amanda lifted Avril from her arms and kissed the baby's forehead. "How was it?" She turned and walked back into the kitchen.

"Wonderful. Just what the doctor ordered to cool off. I love that there's a small beach for the kids." Paige's tummy growled as she stepped inside, spying a bowl of green apples on the granite island. She bit into one and her eyes squeezed into slits at the tart flavor.

"Shhh!" Amanda held up a finger and then pointed at Avril, smiling as she left the room. Julian took a seat next to Paige, slurping loudly on the frozen treat.

He looked up at Paige and his eyes were narrow and serious gazing into hers. "I don't like your bedroom." He pushed the orange ice up the plastic tube and popped a piece into his mouth.

Paige paused mid bite and looked at him. Was it because of the bird or the music box, when she'd been cross with him? "Why not? I like it. It'll be better when the window is fixed." She looked over at the doorway. "I must remember to ask Amanda if she called the people to repair it."

He shook his head, his blue eyes intense above the orange rimmed lips. "That's not it." His gaze dropped for a moment and then he looked up at her. "That box you had yesterday, that music. It's scary, like Scooby Doo ghost scary."

For a moment she could only look at him silently. He wasn't angry with her snapping at him the day before, which was a good thing...but still...

She sighed softly. He was right about the music box. The lure of the music early this morning and the missing block of time wasn't something she could explain. She'd lost almost two hours of time daydreaming about a young woman in a green skirt dancing. That kind of thing had never happened to her before, drifting into some kind of fugue.

She got up and tossed the half-eaten apple in the trash can, her appetite gone now. Forcing a smile, she ruffled his curly locks. There was no need to upset the boy even more than she had the day before. "It's just an old music box. But it may be worth some money and...I don't want you playing with it."

His eyes narrowed, skewering her with his gaze. "That goes for you too, you know."

Her hands flew up in mock surrender. "Alright, alright. Maybe once we're all settled in, I'll take it to an antique store and sell it." She grinned and pinched his thigh, tickling him. "Think of all the freezies I could buy you with that money! A box of them! A crate!"

"A truckload!" He laughed and drained the melted juice from the bottom of the plastic sleeve. "Can I have another one?"

Relief spread through her when he joined in the banter. At least now, he might not have nightmares about the box. When he turned his big blue eyes, the epitome of sad puppy dog up to plead his case for another freezie, her heart melted. "Just one. Don't tell your mom and promise you'll eat a decent lunch after."

She rose from her stool and wandered over to the fridge, popping the freezer door open. She plucked another orange freezie from the open box and slit an opening in the top.

Just in time, she handed him the fresh one, disposed of the used plastic wrapper and scurried to sit down next to him before Amanda walked into the kitchen. Her eyes flitted between them for a few moments before she opened the fridge door. "What would you like for lunch? I was thinking a cold meat sandwich and salad."

Paige looked over at Julian and winked. "Sounds good. Josh is fixing that barn door. After that deer getting in there, he doesn't want any more wildlife taking up residence."

She turned hearing the back door slam open and her mouth fell open seeing Josh step into the room. His face was white as a ghost, and he held his hand at waist level, trying to catch the drips of blood that ran in a rivulet over his palm.

"What the heck happened to you?" Paige reached for the paper towels and handed a sheet to him.

"Josh!" Amanda stepped back from the fridge.

"It's nothing. My own fault. I was chiseling the latch hole, making it deeper so the latch would catch better when the darned thing slipped. I should have been paying more attention." He stepped over to the sink, turned the tap and thrust his bleeding hand into the stream of water.

Paige's gut tightened watching the pink-tinged water drain down the sink. She could feel Julian's eyes watching her, trying to get her attention.

The serious set to Julian's jaw and eyes staring straight into hers made her gut clench tight. It was in that instant that she knew with absolute certainty, what she'd long suspected. Julian was able to sense things, the same way she was—maybe even more so.

Words weren't necessary. Looking into each other's eyes, they knew that the chisel slipping was no accident. There was something in that barn that didn't want them there. The blood dripping from Josh's hand was a warning.

# Chapter Eleven

C 'mon. Let's go get changed before we have lunch. You don't want to get a rash from the damp bathing suit." Paige popped up from the chair and put her hand on Julian's shoulder.

He took a final slurp from the freezie and tossed the wrapper in the trash before stepping alongside her.

As soon as they reached the stairs, out of earshot of the kitchen, she stooped lower, speaking close to him. "Promise me you'll never go into the barn on your own."

He nodded. "Don't worry. But what about Daddy? He shouldn't go in there either."

Paige sighed. Julian had a point. But what could she say to Josh that wouldn't sound totally crazy? Josh was the scientific, engineer type who had to see things to believe them. If she told him the barn had a creepy feeling, and that his accident with the chisel was really no accident, he'd think she was crazy. It wouldn't help the situation when he was counting on her to help with Amanda.

No. This was something she'd have to handle on her own. As long as she could be assured that Julian wouldn't wander in there, it would be okay. Amanda's dream of boarding horses and dogs was waaay down the line. Maybe by then, things in the barn would change. It wasn't something she would worry about right now. After all, worrying is borrowing from the future and paying interest in the present, and her plate was full enough today, thank you.

She put her arm around Julian's shoulder and spoke quietly as they walked up the stairs. From the slump of his shoulders, it was clear he was still worried about his father. "Your dad will be okay, Julian. Sure, he hurt his hand but he's different from you and me."

She hesitated for a moment, looking down at him. "You get weird feelings sometimes, don't you? Sometimes, see the odd thing that other people can't?"

His voice was soft and his eyes welled with tears looking up at her. "Yes. I saw a girl in your room yesterday."

Paige froze and in an instant the image of a girl in a green dress flashed in her mind.

"She saw me watching her and started to come over to me. She looked really mad. That's why I ran away from you yesterday." A tear rolled down his cheek and he edged forward to cling to her, burying his face in her swim cover-up.

It felt like the world was closing in; suddenly she found it hard to breathe as her hand rose to stroke her nephew's back. Julian had seen the girl in the dress? What she'd thought was fear and surprise at her snapping at him was in reality some sort of vision he'd had... of the girl.

It was proof that Julian's gift or sensitivity or whatever name you wanted to use...was actually stronger than her own. He'd been frightened seeing the girl and Paige biting his head off hadn't helped.

"It's okay, Julian. What you saw can't hurt you." She pulled back from him and looked into his eyes, her heart breaking at the quiver in his lower lip and tears falling silently. "I saw her too but it was only in my mind. At least I think it's the same girl. Was she wearing a green dress?"

He nodded. "Yes, she had a dress on, but it was only a little green. She was spooky and kind of white... like on Scooby Doo."

Paige smiled to reassure him. "It doesn't matter. If you see her again, tell me." She started to lead the way up the stairs again but stopped, turning to him once more. "Did you mention this to your mom or dad?"

"No. I knew they'd never believe me and... Mommy would be sad again." His shoulders slumped down and he started to climb the stairs once more.

Paige watched him as he lumbered up the stairs and felt her heart ache. Amanda's depression had been hard on him. He hadn't understood it was a sickness. To him, she was sad and tired all the time. In some ways, Julian had bonded more with her than with his own mother. Hopefully, that was behind them and he'd resume a close relationship with Amanda.

She watched him go into his room and close the door, the weight of the world on his shoulders. She'd have to think of something fun for the two of them to do after lunch...maybe the tire swing again? She sighed and walked down the hall to her own room.

She shimmied out of the damp cover-up dress and then her bathing suit, setting them aside to hang out in the sun to dry. When she opened her dresser to get some dry clothes out, her hand froze on the knob.

The music box that she'd found in the closet was on top of the dresser, sitting squarely in the centre of the white linen table mat! Her heart thundered as she stared at it. The apple in her stomach felt like a lump of lead. There'd been no one in the house for the past couple of hours, yet the box had been moved to her dresser.

She shivered, suddenly aware of cool air on her bare skin. Her hands yanked the drawers open and she grabbed underwear, a T shirt and shorts. Scrambling into the clothes with hands that shook, she looked at the floor keeping her gaze away from the box.

She took a deep breath, and huffed it out fast through flared nostrils. Already she felt stronger, not quite so vulnerable now that she had clothes on. Whatever had moved that box was trying to scare her! It was darned well working, but she couldn't give in to this.

Her eyes narrowed looking at the music box and she lifted it from the dresser. "You don't belong here." She wasn't sure if she was talking to the box or whatever had moved it. Once more the tips of her fingers became numb and tingly as she carried it over to the closet and set it back in the corner.

She stepped out and closed the door, letting her hand linger on the handle for a moment. "Please God, let it stay in there."

At the soft tap on her bedroom door, she jerked back! But it was the other door. She let out a deep breath, striding over to answer it. Julian's eyes were saucer-like as he stood looking up at her. She stepped out of the room and forced a wide smile, steering him gently down the hall at her side.

"Ready for lunch, kiddo?"

He looked up at her and his mouth pulled to the side. "I'm not sure I like it here."

"Give it a chance, Julian. I know it's new for you."

He looked away. "That's not it, Aunt Paige."

"Come on... let's eat." As they tromped down the stairs, she added, "You'll get used to it, don't worry."

He shot her a look. He didn't need to say anything for her to pick up on his answer. Yes, she was a hypocrite but it was for his own good.

# CHAPTER TWELVE

That evening, Paige held a framed portrait of Amanda and her family against the wall next to the flat screen TV. "Here?" She looked over at Amanda, who eyed the position like a hawk on a field mouse.

Julian and Avril were snuggled up on the sofa watching a cartoon movie, while Barney lay sprawled in the doorway.

Amanda shook her head. "Not that one. It's too big for that spot." She reached to grab a smaller print from the stack leaning against the coffee table, and stepping closer, handed it to Paige. "Try this one."

Paige set the first print down and took the one that Amanda extended. This one was her favorite, showing Julian sitting cross-legged on the floor, holding a sleeping newborn Avril. She held it up against the wall and beamed a smile at Amanda. "How's this? Lower, higher?"

Amanda's head tilted forward and she closed one eye. "An inch lower and I'd say it was pretty much perfect."

Paige slipped the pencil from its perch tucked in behind her ear and made a little mark on the wall. She set the picture down and took the hammer, nail and picture hook that Amanda handed to her. When she hammered the nail in with a few sharp taps, Josh's voice could be heard above the TV and the banging.

"All packed up for the week. Hopefully it'll only be a few days but just in case..." He put his arm over Amanda's shoulder and pulled her into his body, giving her a soft kiss on the forehead.

She turned and smiled up at him, her gaze warm and loving. "We should have the internet tomorrow. Maybe then you'll be able to do more work from home."

Paige's chest felt light watching her sister and brother-in-law. The contrast in their looks actually complimented the total effect. With Josh's dark blond hair and fair skin next to her long chestnut hair and olive complexion, they were totally attractive. Or maybe it was because they were still so crazy in love.

"I'm going to try, that's for sure." He smiled half-heartedly.

Paige sighed. There was something happening at work that he had gotten pretty worked up over the other day on the phone. She felt it in her bones that he wasn't going to make it home until at least Friday night.

She glanced at her watch and then looked over at Julian and Avril. It was eight o'clock and way past the toddler's bedtime. They'd been so intent on getting the pictures up that the time had sneaked by like a pickpocket thief.

Stepping over to the sofa, she reached for Avril. "Time for bed, sweetie." There was no resistance from the young child, being lifted in the air. From the droopy eyelids and thumb stuck in her mouth, she was more than ready.

When she stepped closer to Amanda and Josh, they took turns giving Avril a kiss on the cheek and saying goodnight. Amanda smiled and her eyes met her sister's. "Thanks, Paige."

Actually, it was no big hardship to take Avril up to bed and get her tucked in for the night. It was one of her favorite things, snuggling a little in the small bed while the little girl drifted off to sleep.

She walked up the wide set of stairs and turned into the bedroom, flipping the light switch as she walked past it. After setting the tyke down on the bed, she grabbed the change pad, a fresh diaper and her pajamas from the bottom drawer of the change table.

Paige lowered to her knees and tugged Avril's T shirt up and over her head. The child was now fully awake, flipping onto her side and looking at the space behind Paige, burbling with delight. Once more the little girl's head bobbed higher, eyes dancing while gazing at the closet. She let out a squeal of laughter, squirming higher still.

"Hey, silly Willie! What's so funny?" Paige slipped the pajama top onto Avril's head and tugged it down.

Avril grinned and peeked around Paige's legs, pointing her finger. "Her! She's funny."

Goosebumps skittered down Paige's arms and the smile on her lips vanished like mist. Oh my God. Avril was playing peek-a-boo with something or someone behind her. Paige held the child's waist with both of her hands and turned her head slowly to look behind her.

There was only the door standing ajar, revealing the dark inner space of the closet. Her eyes squinted trying to see into the darkness. Still nothing.

At the low growl coming from the other direction, Paige jerked. Her mouth fell open seeing Barney standing in the doorway, the hackles making his hair stand straight in a thick line down his back. His lips were curled in a snarl, revealing sharp, white fangs, his eyes focused on the closet.

She blinked a couple of times, hardly trusting her eyes. Barney never looked this ferocious! Her heart hammered a mile a minute in her chest. Oh God. The growl became a fierce bark, his glaring eyes never leaving the dark yawn of the closet. There had to be something there...something he and Avril could see.

Pulling Avril close, she was about to scramble to her feet when Josh and Amanda whipped into the room.

"Easy Barney. Stop." Josh petted the dog's head and stared wide-eyed at Paige. "What's going on?"

Paige scurried to the door carrying Avril firmly in her arms. "The closet. You'd better check it."

"Oh my God, another break-in! I thought we'd be safe here!" Amanda reached for Avril and fled the room, her feet thudding quickly down the stairs.

Josh's jaw muscle worked as he reached for Barney's collar. "C'mon, boy."

But Barney stood his ground, feet planted and another low growl rumbled in his chest. Josh looked around the room, searching for something. "Shit!" He grabbed the jar of cotton balls from the change table, and holding it above his head ready to fling it, stepped slowly to the closet.

The whole time that he advanced to the dark opening, Paige stood still as a statue in the doorway, barely daring to breathe. Yet even as she stood there, she knew before Josh flipped the closet light on, that there wouldn't be anything there—certainly not anything that Josh could clobber with a jar of cotton balls.

She looked down at Barney and saw his hackles lower and his stump of a tail begin to wag. Peering at Josh, the words rushed out, "Avril saw something and then Barney—"

"Was this it?" Josh reached down and picked up a doll from the floor in the closet.

The doll's glass eyes blinked open and then stared blindly over at Paige.

"No Josh! Avril wouldn't play peek-a-boo with *that!* Besides, it was dark in there. What about Barney? He wouldn't growl at a doll." Paige stepped closer to Josh, her chin leading the way. She'd had enough spooky things scaring her and for Josh to be so matter of fact, holding the doll up to explain everything...well, it was insulting.

Josh turned and his hand swept the air. "Well? What else could it be? There's only her clothes hanging there and some toys." He sighed and stepped by her, pushing Barney with his knee. "Get out of here, you goof. Scaring everyone like that. Especially Amanda. Great."

He turned to Paige and rolled his eyes. "He must have heard a mouse or something. Something we can't hear. That's the only logical explanation." He tossed the doll on the bed and left the room.

Paige took a deep breath and blew it out slowly through puffed cheeks. If only he was right. But the cold knot in her gut screamed otherwise.

# CHAPTER THIRTEEN

The next morning, the sound of rain thrumming on the window seeped into Paige's consciousness. She'd just managed to get to sleep after a restless night and now the dim light and the noise penetrating the room woke her. No. Just five more minutes. She snuggled deeper into the warm bed, tugging the comforter over her head.

But the thud of feet racing down the hall to her door wasn't about to let that happen. She sighed and threw the comforter off and rolled out of her sleepy nest.

"Shush! Kids! Let her sleep." Amanda's muffled voice and footsteps followed.

Paige slipped her robe on and opened the bedroom door, blinking the sleep from her eyes. Julian and Avril, still in their pajamas, stood at her door with shy grins looking up at her while Amanda raced behind, reaching for them.

"Sorry, Paige." Amanda's teeth bit gently down on her lower lip.

Paige stifled a yawn and stepped out of the room. "It's okay. Has Josh left yet?" She ruffled Julian's hair and bent to scoop Avril into her arms.

Amanda called over her shoulder. "Yeah, about a half hour ago. Now that you're up, I'm going to grab a quick shower and get dressed." She disappeared inside her bedroom.

"Aunt Paige, do you want to play a game? Maybe Snakes and Ladders or Jenga?" Julian tugged at her robe.

She took a deep breath and smiled down at him. "I'm not doing anything until I've had a cup of coffee. I take it, you two have eaten." She started down the hall, with Julian on her heels like a puppy.

"Yeah. We were up early to see Daddy before he left. What are we going to do today? I hate rain. We could watch movies or play video games." Julian kept up a steady chatter as they walked down the stairs.

"How about I set the TV up with a movie for you, while I have breakfast and then get ready for the day? How does that sound?" Without waiting for an answer Paige led the way into the living room and plopped Avril down onto the sofa.

"How about this one?" Julian held out a DVD with a picture of cartoon cars and trucks.

She took it and popped it into the player and turned on the TV. As it flickered to life she glanced to the wall where she had hung the picture of Julian and Avril.

The smile fell from her lips and her face tightened. The photo was still there but now, it was sideways, barely hanging on at the corner of the frame. She would have sworn she'd set the metal hook at the back of the picture over the prong of the hanger. But even if she hadn't, how could it slip to that degree? A banging door wouldn't cause it to slide *that* far.

She took a deep breath and straightened the picture. Maybe one of the kids knocked it with some toy...or Josh bumped into it...That must have been what happened.

The movie started up and she smiled at the kids curled up on the sofa watching the TV screen. They looked so cozy and innocent, already engrossed in a movie they'd probably seen a hundred times. Even Julian was unconcerned with anything but what was playing on the screen. If she had anything to say about it, that was the way it would stay.

She left the room and wandered through the dining room into the kitchen. The only evidence that Josh had even been there was his coffee cup in the sink next to the kids' cereal bowls and juice glasses.

The dog rose to its feet and ambled over, waiting for her to open the fridge and share a treat. His large yap was open, tongue lolling to the side and his eyes were bright watching her. He was the same old Barney, the happy beggar ensuring that no one forgot to slip him a hunk of cheese or slice of cold meat while they were busy in the kitchen. If she hadn't seen him snarling with fangs bared last night, she would never have believed it could be the same dog.

"Here Barney. Let me get you a nice treat." She went to the pantry and fished a Milk Bone from the bag sitting on the shelf. He sniffed it and as gentle as a lamb he pulled the biscuit from her fingers. "Good boy."

She went to the cabinet, got a mug and poured a cup of coffee. As she sipped, she looked out the back window that overlooked the yard. The rain was letting up a bit and the sky looked brighter than earlier. She squinted trying to see across the yard to the barn. The doors were shut tight, nudged closed by a large rock set up against them.

"Thanks, Josh." She smiled and took a seat at the island, pulling her cell phone from the pocket of her robe. No texts or messages from her friends. She sighed and her thumbs flew sending a message to Jennifer, letting her know that the move went well and they were just about settled in.

She set the phone down and rose to her feet to get another coffee and something to eat. When she reached into the cabinet for a bowl, the doorbell rang and Barney barked, racing to the front door. She sighed and followed him, wondering who could be at the door at that hour of the day.

After peeking out the side panel and seeing a cable communications van, she opened the door. Amanda had said that the internet and satellite TV was due to be hooked up. Great. She'd be able to stream movies and stay in touch with everyone on social media.

The young guy who stared back made her eyes flare wide for just a moment. Oh my God. He had the deepest blue eyes and cutest smile! And his tanned muscular arms and wide set of shoulders weren't hard on the eyes either. Her hand flew to the opening of her robe, fingers spread along her chest and neck. If she'd known a guy this ripped and good looking would be there to install the internet, she'd have at *least* washed her face.

"Hi. Mrs. Jenkins?" There was even a dimple in his cheek when he smiled.

"No. I'm Paige, her sister. You're here for the TV and satellite, right? You're here to hook up? That's it, right?" What was wrong with her mouth, stammering like she'd never seen a guy this gorgeous before? It was just that she'd never expected to see one way out in the middle of nowhere. Oh shit! Did she just ask him if he was here to hook up? Aaaa!

"Aunt Paige?" Avril's arm slipped around her legs, and her cheek rested against the side of her thigh.

She patted the little girl's back and looked down. "It's okay sweetie. Go watch the movie with Julian. I'll be just a minute."

When Avril grinned and walked back to the living room, Paige's gaze was once more captive to the cable guy.

"Cute kid. I'm Matt Hawley. There's a satellite on the west side of the house that I'll reconnect for you. I installed it for the last owners. I brought a new receiver for you. Do you mind if I come inside and check the wire?" He flashed a smile and peeked past her into the large foyer.

"No. For sure." Paige stepped back holding the door wider for him to enter. Her gaze fell to the dark blue shorts and golden muscular calves and work boots. He had to be at least six feet four, with a dark mane of hair most girls would give their eye teeth for.

He cleared his throat and looked around at the high ceilings and wood-work. "Wow. They sure did a great job on this place." He glanced over at her. "The Partridges, I mean. Although it was no big surprise when they left after just a few months."

"Yeah, of course." Paige's arms crossed over her chest and she stepped closer to him. "They were in the military and had to take a transfer. The real estate company told my sister all about it."

He chuckled and his hand rose to rub the back of his neck while he looked down at the floor. "That's what they said, huh? Funny. The hus-band was in his late forties. Kind of old for a transfer." He smiled and stepped into the living room. "But if that's what they told you, who am I to say different?"

Paige followed him into the room, her gut tightening as she watched him. "What do you mean, no big surprise that they left? It wasn't a transfer?" There was more that he knew about all of this; she could tell by the skeptical glint of his eye.

"Well..." He hesitated, looking at the kids, who were staring wide eyed at him, their cartoon forgotten.

At Amanda's footsteps on the stairs, he looked past Paige out to the foyer.

Amanda stepped into the room and grinned. "Great! You're the cable guy, right? Not that you look anything like the TV cable guy, that Larry, but—"

"Amanda. This is Matt. He knew the Partridges. He installed the satellite for them." Paige interrupted, trying to get back on topic.

"Oh yeah?" Amanda picked the remote up and paused the cartoon. She looked down at Julian and Avril. "Time for you two to get dressed. You can finish this movie after that." She gestured for them to get up and then turned to Matt, "We'll get these guys out of your way." She smiled and then she and the big black dog followed the kids out of the room and up the stairs.

Matt shrugged his shoulders and then bent down to check the cable box and wire coming into it.

"What were you starting to tell me before my sister came in?" Paige's eyes narrowed as she moved across the room to stand over him. She scooped her hair to one side holding it in her hand peering down at him.

He rose and the smile was gone from his face when he spoke. "Look, I grew up not far from here. Actually, I bought a place across the lake, so I'm pretty familiar with the area."

Paige pulled the edges of her robe tighter together, fisting the collar at her neck. "So you know this house, the barn and the acreage? Know who built it, who lived here?"

Matt didn't answer right away. He stepped closer to the window and looked up at the sky where a beam of sunshine pierced through the clouds.

He shrugged and turned to her, "I've got to check the line and the dish now. C'mon outside with me. We can talk there." He looked around the living room, from the high ceiling to the hardwood floor and sighed before striding out the door.

She paused for a moment. The fact he wanted to speak to her outside added fuel to the worry in her gut. She fought off the sudden tightness in her stomach and instead, took a deep breath, squaring her shoulders. She had to find out more about this house that Amanda had bought. There was something weird about it...even Julian sensed it.

This guy, Matt, could probably fill in some of the blanks.

# CHAPTER FOURTEEN

O utside, the wet grass was cold on her bare feet when she hurried over to where he stood in the open hatch at the back of the van. He reached in and took out a gadget and toyed with it, before looking over at her. "This house...it's got a reputation. Some people say it's haunted."

"Oh my God." She hugged her arms across her body, her fingers grasping the cotton robe tightly. "That's crazy! It's a bit eerie, I'll give you that...but actually *haunted*? That's a bit far-fetched." But Julian seeing that girl in her bedroom niggled, denying the forced optimism.

He shook his head and sighed. "I don't believe in all that crap, of course. It's just that..." He pushed the bill of the ball cap higher, revealing a lock of dark hair, like a comma on his forehead. "I probably shouldn't say any more. It's idle gossip and you and your sister don't need to hear it."

Paige rolled her eyes and huffed a sigh. "Look, you started this, so at least finish it. Okay?"

He looked at the ground silently for a moment before reaching up to unhook the ladder from the roof of the van. "People move in here but they never stay very long. The Partridges probably had the house longer than most..." He shoved a couple of tools into his leather work belt and hoisted the ladder down. "...whatever it is about this house, people leave, in a real hurry."

Paige could feel the muscles in the back of her neck tighten watching Matt shrug and then walk away to the side of the house where the satellite dish was mounted. The guy might be good looking as hell but she could clobber him with all his cryptic clues and innuendos.

"Hey Matt?" She called after him and then hurried to catch up. He smiled and she returned the gesture. "People say it's haunted, right?"

He nodded slowly and his eyes narrowed watching her.

It was hard to keep the shock from showing on her face. But she needed to hear more and playing dumb seemed like the best route.

"What people? Do you know anyone who actually has some concrete knowledge about this place or is it all just rumors and conjecture—stories that amuse the locals at Halloween?" She smiled to take the sting out of her words. From the droop of his shoulders, she'd scored a point.

"You really want to know, huh?" He adjusted the ladder taking some of its weight on his thigh before his mouth set in a tight line. "My aunt knows about this house. Well actually she's my great-aunt. She still works in the library a couple days a week but she used to teach school years and years ago in the village."

"So *she* told you about it?" Paige leaned closer, watching him with wide eyes. This was great. Now she'd finally find out what the heck was going on in that house and how she was going to...

She jerked back as the realization hit her, finishing the thought...*how she was going to protect them*. The fortune teller's words rang in her head. '*Protect yourself*.'

Matt shook his head. "No. She clams up whenever anyone talks about the house." His gaze bore into her eyes and roamed over her face. "Are you okay? You look like you've seen a ghost." He grimaced, his face coloring with embarrassment. "Sorry, wasn't trying to be funny considering the conversation and all."

She took a deep breath and forced a smile. "No, my mind wandered for a few seconds. I'd like to talk to your aunt. What's her name? Does she live in the village? Can you give me her phone number?"

He chuckled and held his hand up like a traffic control cop. "Hold on! I'm not sure she'll talk to you about the house considering she doesn't talk to anyone about it, but..." His cheeks turned pinker and he looked down at the ground for a moment. "You'd have a better chance, if I take you over to meet her."

It was then that Paige noticed his fingers and the fact that there was no ring there. No wonder he looked embarrassed. If she didn't know better, she'd swear he'd been mysterious about the house, angling for a date. But what normal, good-looking guy has to contrive to get a date when it's at his great aunt's? Nah.

She smiled and felt her own cheeks flush warmly. "That would be nice. I mean, I would really appreciate it...talking to your aunt. What'd you say her name was?" Once more her hand clasped the edges of her robe tight to her neck.

"Barbara Hawley, same last name as me. She's on my dad's side and never married." He looked over at the satellite dish that was mounted on a thick pole protruding from the ground. He put the ladder against it and looked at her, then up at the dish.

Her eyes went wide following his gaze and seeing the hint for what it was. "You've got work to do, I'm sorry that I'm keeping you from it. Just let me know when and where and we can meet up to see your aunt." She started to turn, mumbling, "I'd better go in and get dressed." Paige's heart had sped up a little, but this time it wasn't from anything in the house.

"Wait. Sure, I'll set it up." He set the ladder down and scooped his cell phone from his pocket. "What's your number?"

She watched him as she dictated her cell number, and he keyed it in. A small smile lit his face as he entered the information, looking down at the gadget.

When he was done, she felt her cheeks warm and stammered, "I'd better go in." As she walked away, she glanced back over her shoulder at him. He just happened to be looking her way as well.

She smiled back and went into the house.

# Chapter Fifteen

S he was about to walk up the stairs, but glanced in the living room. Her breath caught in her throat and she stopped dead in her tracks. Amanda stood near the wall, adjusting the picture of the kids, the one that she fixed earlier.

Her mouth went suddenly dry and her voice kind of croaked, "What is *with* that picture?"

Amanda's hand lifted and she turned, flashing a warm smile. "There. What do you mean what's with it? It was crooked, that's all." She stepped past the kids who were setting up a tower of Jenga blocks on the floor. "That cable guy's cute, eh?"

Paige decided to let the picture issue go. Amanda was so casual about it there was no use making a fuss and upsetting her. Besides, she'd probably be interested in hearing about the 'date' with Matt. "Yeah, he is. He asked for my phone number. How do you like that?"

Amanda scurried over and gripped her arm. "*Get out*! He hit on you?" Her eyes were fairly dancing with excitement, the grin a mile wide.

"Yup. Guess I still got it, huh?" Paige smirked and then sashayed up the stairs, swinging her hips, doing a total vamp. Behind her Amanda squee'd like a school girl. It was funny. This was the first guy she'd actually noticed in a long time and it was because of her sister's creepy house—not that she'd get into that angle with Amanda.

She hurried down the hallway. With any luck she'd be able to get in a fast shower and get dressed before Matt left. She wouldn't mind getting his number as well.

The tinny bell note of the music box sounded softly in the air. Paige jerked to a stop, her mouth falling open. Oh my God. She leaned forward, creeping softly the rest of the way to her room. More notes of the melancholy song filled the air, sending a shiver up her spine.

Inside the room, in the centre of her bed, was the music box, lid open, playing the ancient song. She could only stare at it, her hands clutching the robe at her neck. Her heart pounded like a hammer drill and the breath caught in her chest. With narrow eyes she saw a golden glint flash from the brass tube, catching the light on its tiny barbs lifting the keys.

She darted forward and slammed the lid shut, her fingers fumbling for the key mechanism at the back to stop it. The silence that followed was thick, her fingers tingling as she held the box before her chest. Her gaze flitted around the room. Twice, the box had been moved. The only other person who knew about the box was Julian. There was no way he'd touch it. He said it frightened him.

This time, the box sitting there on her bed was worse than the dresser. It felt personal now. There was no way she was ever going to sleep in that room again if that box was still in it. She had to get it out of there, but where could she put it?

It was absolutely too creepy to be in the house. There was no way that the kids should find it, to play it and as for Amanda...Something told her that her sister wouldn't understand, not the way she and Julian understood.

She bent down and pulled the suitcase out from under her bed. Inside it was her carry-on bag. She grabbed it and flipped the lid open, setting the music box inside. She zipped it closed and then fastened the buckles for good measure. It could stay in her car and the first chance she got to go into the city to visit an antique store, she'd get rid of the blasted thing.

She set the suitcase next to the door and peered at the closet and then slowly her gaze wandered over the rest of the room. It was one thing to get the music box out of the house but there was still something lurking, which had moved it. What would she do to deal with that?

Hopefully after talking to Matt's great aunt, she'd have a better idea.

# CHAPTER SIXTEEN

Later that day, Paige sat down at the kitchen island booting up her laptop. The house was quiet as a morgue. Amanda and Julian were on a hike exploring the lakeside, and Avril was upstairs having a nap. Even the dog was quiet, choosing to sleep next to Avril's bed, rather than go on the hike.

She bit into an apple, munching while she typed her password. Three days without the internet and social media was like a lifetime. After reading and replying to the emails from her friends in Toronto, she pulled her cell phone out of her pocket. In a few minutes the connection was registered and the photo files she'd taken when they'd arrived, transferred over onto the laptop. The one she'd taken of the kids on the tire swing had been cute. She would send that along to Amanda and Josh.

When she clicked the photo file open, it filled the screen. Her breath froze in chest when she looked at the picture. What the hell? Julian was smiling, gently pushing his sister on the tire swing but what was behind him made goose bumps skitter up her arms.

The form of a young girl, wispy and ethereal hovered behind the little boy. But the girl's eyes...she felt the hair on the back of her neck tingle, when she peered at the red slits. Such rage, an evil malevolence peering beyond Julian and Avril into the camera lens made her heart leap into a fast gallop.

THUD!

She jumped up from her chair, almost upsetting the laptop. It had come from upstairs! Barney's barks and growls were followed by a high-pitched shriek. Avril!

Paige raced through the house to get to the stairs, taking them two at a time.

When she entered the room, Avril was huddled in the top corner of her bed against the wall, cowering. Barney snarled and snapped staring at the closet. The centre ridge of hair on his back bristled straight up. Oh my God. The change table dresser was laying on its side next to the dog. Diapers, baby wipes and paper towels were scattered across the floor.

"Easy boy! Barney, hush." Paige patted the dog's wiry hair stepping by him to reach across the bed for Avril.

The little girl's eyes were bulging marbles when she turned and then scurried into her arms. Paige hugged her, rolling her hand gently over the toddler's back. "There, there. It's okay." She stepped out of the room and hurried down the stairs. She could hear the dog's nails click on the wood floor behind her.

She settled onto the kitchen chair, rocking the small child back and forth on her lap. The dog was content to lay next to them, panting a bit before resting its head on the cool floor. Now that they were downstairs and quiet had once more descended, Paige willed her heart to slow, taking long, slow breaths.

The change table falling over was obviously what woke Avril up. And scared the hell out of her! Had Barney somehow caused it to fall? Her stomach fell, as the hard truth sunk in. The dog had nothing to do with that table falling. It was more likely he'd been startled awake as well.

Just like the night before, there was something about that closet that really bugged him. She snorted. Something that got his hackles up *for real*. And Avril...she had said there was a girl in the closet, someone making her laugh.

Paige stroked the child's long, silky hair with one hand and with the other she tapped the mouse pad of her laptop, waking it from the screensaver snooze.

"Avril? Are you okay now?" She pulled back from the little girl's head and looked down at her. Her dark eyes were wide above the thumb firmly planted in her mouth, but she managed a nod.

Paige turned slightly in her chair, so that her niece could see the computer screen. "Avril? See my laptop? Was this the girl you saw in your closet last night?"

Avril's gaze shifted to the laptop. "Yes." She turned her head, burying her face into the curve of Paige's neck.

Paige held the child closer, once more brushing her hand over her hair. Oh my God. The poor kid, seeing that thing in her room. That specter hiding in her closet. It was no wonder the dog went so nuts...he sensed it as well. There was no way the poor little kid was ever going to sleep in there--

At the sound of Julian's voice and the back door opening, Paige swiveled in her chair to face her sister.

Amanda's head tilted to the side when she saw Paige holding Avril. "Is anything wrong?" She stepped over and Avril squirmed away from Paige, reaching up for her mother.

Julian met Paige's gaze and then stood beside her looking at the picture on the laptop. His hand clutched at her thigh, but Paige continued, turning the laptop slightly so that Amanda could see it.

"Amanda, we need to talk. "

"What the..." Her sister leaned closer so she could take a better look, squinting her eyes. "Tell me that's some kind of trick caused by the light. ..or some kind of double exposure?" She pulled a chair out from the island and sank down into it, still holding Avril in her arms.

Julian whispered, his eyes wide looking up at Paige, "That's her. That's the girl in your room."

"*What*?" Amanda reached for his arm, tugging until he swiveled to face her. "Julian, you *saw* this girl?" Her eyes sparked at Paige. "How is this possible? You did something didn't you? You're good with that kind of software. You tinkered with the pictures." She huffed a sigh and frowned. "This isn't funny, Paige!"

"No, Amanda, I swear, didn't do anything with that photo." Paige pushed the laptop farther away and reached down to lift Julian onto her lap. She sighed. Where could she start? She couldn't hide this from Amanda any longer.

Of course, Amanda would be like Josh in all likelihood, not believing or even trying to understand but she had to try. Just because Josh and Amanda always looked for the most logical rational explanation for things, didn't mean that there *was* one.

"Amanda..." She paused and looked down at the table for a moment, trying to plan her next words. "I think this thing in the photo, this girl...is a ghost. She haunts this house and maybe even the barn."

Amanda shook her head and her lips twitched nervously in a smile before kissing the top of Avril's head. "No. That's crazy, Paige."

"No, it isn't. I hate to say this but, I'm pretty sure Avril saw this girl last night in her closet. Barney acts like he can see her too, going all junk-yard dog, psycho."

Julian's voice was high and his eyes were round watching his mother. "I saw her too, Mommy. She was in Aunt Paige's room yesterday. She was coming towards me and I ran!"

"I don't believe it." Amanda's chin rose and she shook her head quickly. "First of all, there's no such thing as ghosts and even if there were, they would have told us when we looked at the house. I think there's something in their code of ethics that makes them tell people if there's something weird about a house." She snorted and continued rocking back and forth on the chair with Avril clinging to her, the child sucking her thumb with renewed energy.

Paige's arms felt like lead holding Julian and watching the smirk on Amanda's face. But she had to give it one more try at least. "Apparently this house has a reputation with the locals. That's what I was talking to Matt about this morning. He's going to take me to see his aunt. She knows the whole story about the house."

Julian tugged at Paige's arm. "Tell her about the music box and the barn."

Paige sighed. She had wanted to do this a little at a time, try to convince Amanda slowly, not bowl her over with everything at once.

"What *about* the barn?" Amanda rose to her feet and wandered over to the window, staring out towards the dark building.

"There's nothing concrete, okay? It's more a feeling that there's something in there. Something watching us. And the door banged shut that first day here. I don't think it was the deer, like Josh said." Paige sighed. "We need to find out more about the house and its history. Maybe a priest needs to bless the house or something."

After Amanda set Avril down onto the floor, her eyes narrowed and she took a deep breath. "Josh and I haven't experienced anything weird with the house—not when we first looked at it and even now, *nothing odd*. The photo is weird, I'll grant you that, but a ghost? It's pretty faded and the red eyes could be a trick of the sunlight. Maybe it caught a leaf that's already turned to an autumn color."

Paige couldn't believe her ears listening to her sister, watching her casually saunter over to the fridge and get a couple of frozen treats out for the kids. Amanda was just like Josh, striving to find any logical explanation. Even the fear on Julian's and Avril's face hadn't moved her.

She leaned forward, her arms planted firmly on the island table, "Amanda. The dressing table in Avril's room was knocked over. That's what woke her. Barney was going berserk barking at the closet. I think--"

Amanda held her finger high, silencing Paige. She turned to Julian, "How about you two go play in the living room so Aunt Paige and I can talk." She smiled at Julian, handing him the frozen treats.

He took the red sleeve of sweet ice and then looked over at Paige for a few moments before he turned to his sister. "C'mon Avril. Let's go."

There'd been a silent plea in his eye when he looked at Paige. But what was he hoping for—to go along with Amanda's false confidence or stay true to the fact that there was something very wrong with the house. There wasn't much time to deliberate it as Amanda took a seat across from her and began speaking again.

"Paige, the house is old and I suppose, it could be considered spooky. In some ways it reminds me of Grandma's house in Cobourg. Do you remember it? You were only seven when she died. Grandpa sold it to move closer to us after that. You were always afraid to go into the attic, even though there were trunks of wonderful old clothes to play dress-up with."

Paige's mouth fell open watching Amanda sitting so placidly. She hadn't thought of that old farmhouse in years. A flash of her twelve-year-old sister, her long dark braids swirling out as she rounded the narrow staircase leading to the attic, played in Paige's mind. The only time Amanda had succeeded in talking her into going up to the attic, Paige had seen white orbs of light floating near the antique trunks. She'd stared, feeling dread and heaviness fill her body, before racing back down the stairs.

It *had* been haunted up there. Even Grandma Sarah had said so when she tucked her in that night. She said it was a secret that Amanda would never understand and to stay away from the attic. She'd also warned her to never go anywhere near the old well. Of course, there was always the risk of falling into it but there was more to it than that. Something about dark power and some lines running through the earth.

So the fact that Amanda was defending the house, really shouldn't surprise her. She'd never sensed anything supernatural before. It was one thing that Josh and Amanda were totally in sync with. Their minds were closed about the possibility of there being anything else in the universe besides what you could actually touch or see.

Paige's chin rose and she sat straighter in the chair, "I remember Grandma's. I remember it was haunted even though you didn't believe it. Amanda. There's something wrong here, in this house. I'm going to find out what it is and then I'm going to fix it."

She grabbed her laptop and stormed out of the kitchen to join the kids and make sure they were all right. As she crossed the hallway, she noticed Barney sprawled in the doorway. It looked like he had the same idea.

# CHAPTER SEVENTEEN

The kids were coloring in their books, the bright markers scattered in a pile between them, where they lay on the floor. Julian got to his feet when Paige entered and the two of them sat close together on the sofa.

"Mommy doesn't see what we see, Aunt Paige." He glanced over at the laptop which was still open displaying the scene at the tire swing. "That girl looks mad. Why would she be mad at us?" He nestled in closer to Paige's side, his gaze never leaving the screen of the laptop.

There was a lump in the back of her throat looking down at him. He was so sweet and innocent trying to figure this out. "I don't know, Julian. But I don't think she's mad at you, but rather mad because she used to live here, like us. And now it's like she's trapped here when she should have left."

He looked up at her and his eyes filled with tears. "I think she used to sleep in your room. The bird that broke the window...I wasn't supposed to be in that room. You were."

The hair on Paige's head and neck tingled and she closed her laptop with a snap. Whatever was here, Julian had a much better sense of its nature than she did. "When we were near the barn the other day, was it this girl you sensed in there?"

He shook his head and then looked down at his lap. "No. That's something else in there. Something really old—a man." A tear fell onto his hand and he smeared it on his pants. "I need to go to the bathroom. Will you come with me?"

Paige looked down at Avril who was busy filling in the dress of a Disney princess, the tip of her tongue curled in the corner of her mouth. "It's okay, Jules. Your Mom's in the kitchen right next to it. You'll be fine." She got up and held out her hand, tugging him to his feet.

When he left the room. Paige glanced over at the picture hanging next to the TV. Her eyebrows rose and she sighed with relief seeing it the way it had been left earlier—hanging straight. She squatted down next to Avril and began coloring the opposite page. "Good job, Avril. You're staying inside the lines."

There were still some boxes sitting on the far end of the room that were ready to be un-packed but this was more important right then. Doing something normal and mundane like coloring to get Avril past the earlier shock.

Oh God, that room. Even with Barney sleeping on the floor next to Avril, it wasn't enough to protect her. This girl ghost wasn't going to be put off by the dog or anything, just showing up and scaring the dickens out of everyone. And the dresser falling over? Someone could have been seriously hurt. There was no way she was going to let Avril sleep in there on her own anymore. She'd stay in there with her until things got sorted out.

Her gut churned. But what if they didn't? What then?

The sounds of Amanda working in the kitchen doing dinner prep and tidying up drifted into the living room. She sighed and her hand moved slowly, coloring the page. She didn't want to fight with Amanda but her sister wasn't taking any of this seriously enough.

When Julian entered the room again, Paige smiled and got to her feet. While he moved off to the upholstered chair near the window, turning the small black tablet on to play a game, Paige settled on the sofa. She opened the laptop and typed in the search bar 'protecting yourself from ghosts and evil spirits'

Her eyes widened seeing the screen fill with hits—everything from Wiccan spells to herbs and prayers in the suggested links. She opened a few and spent the next while reading about sea salt, candles, prayers and holy water.

When Avril popped up to her feet, holding the picture she'd just finished coloring, Paige's head jerked back. Avril's picture was your typical Disney princess with the frothy pink dress and golden hair but she'd had done the eyes a fiery red. Paige's gut tightened, while her eyes flitted from the picture to Avril's smile. "Nice coloring, but Belle's eyes are supposed to be brown, Avril."

Avril giggled and turned the book to look at the page again. "Cora did it. She has red eyes and she wanted Belle to have red eyes too."

Paige's heart pounded hard in her chest. Cora? This girl or ghost had communicated with Avril? She knew its name?

She looked up at the picture hanging near the TV and gasped. Once more it was tilted, held only by the corner of the frame. Oh my God.

# CHAPTER EIGHTEEN

Amanda appeared in the doorway, flipping the dishtowel over her shoulder. "I made some brownies for dessert tonight."

Paige gaped at her sister. The air in the living room had suddenly become chilly and...and somehow, *thick*. She found it hard to breathe. Brownies were the last thing she needed, as she peered down at the picture in Avril's book.

This thing, or this girl, had been there! She'd been right next to Avril while she colored! And just to make sure that there was no doubt about her visit, she'd messed with the picture hanging on the wall...*again*!

"What's with you Paige? You look like you've seen a—"

"*Ghost*, Amanda? Yeah. She was right here in this room with us, coloring with Avril! Look at the picture on the wall, Amanda! Think I did that? Think again." Paige hardly ever raised her voice to her sister and the look of surprise on Amanda's face made that clear.

"Mommy?"

Amanda looked over at Julian who was tucked into the overstuffed chair, looking back like a deer in the headlights.

Avril zipped past her mother and her small feet clamored quickly up the stairs. Amanda turned and took a few steps following her. "Avril! Come back here. Where're you going?"

Paige raced across the room to the door, dodging by her sister. "Avril! Stop!"

With the dog following closely on her heels, Paige rounded the newel post and stepped into Avril's room in time to see the little girl disappear inside the closet. The door behind Avril, banged shut so hard the floor shuddered. Paige stepped by the change table that was still strewn on its side and reached for the door knob.

"Avril? Come out. What are you doing?" Paige twisted the knob and pulled but the door wouldn't budge. It wasn't locked, not from the way the knob moved. But there was no way it was opening. Something was holding it tight!

Amanda's footsteps sounded over the dog's low, rumbling snarls.

"Paige! What's she doing? Where is she?"

Paige's head spun and she saw her own fear mirrored in her sister's face, "Help me, Amanda! She's in the closet and I can't get the door open!"

She turned back and the door flew open on its own. It happened so quickly, she stumbled back a step, but caught herself before she fell to the floor. With round eyes she stared into the closet where Avril stood looking shyly up at her mother.

"Avril! What are you doing, hiding in the closet? You scared your Aunt Paige and me." This time it was Amanda who brushed Paige's shoulder on her way to scoop up the tyke. "What were you thinking?"

"It was Cora." At Julian's low voice, Paige spun to face him.

A dark wet stain spread from the crotch of his jeans to his knees. Tears blurred his eyes and then he slumped down onto the floor, falling onto his side.

She rushed over and gasped when she saw his closed eyes. She shook his shoulder. "Julian! C'mon Julian! What's wrong?"

There was nothing, no movement at all. His eyes were shut and he was sound asleep, breathing gently.

"What's *wrong* with him?" Amanda handed Avril to Paige and she reached for her son. "Julian!"

BANG!

The closet door behind them shut with such force that the walls shook.

"We've got to get out of here! Quick! Pick him up, Amanda!" Paige led the way out into the hall, and stood peering into the room.

Amanda, with her hands clutching Julian stumbled forward into the hallway. Her eyes squeezed shut and she hugged her son. "Julian! Oh my God!"

Barney gave a final, pained yip before racing from the room. With the toddler clinging, her tiny arms and legs tight around her body, Paige darted over to yank the bedroom door shut. Her heart was racing and for a moment she felt faint. Oh my God, this couldn't really be happening. It was a nightmare!

"Julian! Wake up!" Amanda looked over at her sister. "*Paige!* What's wrong with him? We've got to get him to the hospital! He won't wake up! What the hell is going on?"

She held him firmly with one arm curled over his body, gripping the banister with the other, descending the stairs quickly. Paige was right behind her.

"Mommy?"

Paige gasped at the sound of the boy's voice. It was so weak!

"Oh my God! Julian! My baby! You're all right?" Amanda paused and slumped down onto the stair, holding her son in her lap, blinking back the tears.

"It touched me. It went right through me. It was cold, like ice inside my tummy." Julian's voice was soft and tears flowed down his cheek looking up at his mother. He turned to Paige. "It was her—Cora."

The hair on Paige's neck tingled and her chest felt like iron bands circled it, getting tighter and tighter. She held Avril close and glanced behind her. Where was this Cora now? She wasn't still in Avril's room; Julian had felt her leave it.

"Paige? What just happened here?" Amanda's voice trailed off and she shook her head slowly. "Oh God...I don't understand."

Paige looked down at her sister and her jaw tightened. "Neither do I, believe me. Come on. We can't stay here on the stairs. Let's go into the kitchen." There was something about salt that she'd read earlier.

She followed Amanda down and darted into the living room to grab her laptop. As she passed by the front door, she fought the urge to race out, get in her car and drive, leave all the scary shit behind. But this was Amanda's home now. It wasn't just as simple as driving away. The kids needed her.

When she entered the kitchen, Julian was sitting at the island, drinking a glass of water. He turned his big blue eyes up at her when she set Avril on the chair next to him. "What did you do with the music box, Aunt Paige? Cora is mad that you took it. She wants it back."

Avril nodded as well. Paige froze

"What's he talking about Paige? What music box?" Amanda gave Avril a glass of water and scowled. She sunk down into the other chair and her face was tight gazing at Paige.

Paige huffed a sigh setting the laptop on the island. This whole dramatic show—the banging doors, Cora's 'visitation' next to Avril, messing with

Avril's coloring, and the picture hanging askew...it was all done to make a point.

Cora was pissed.

She gritted her teeth and tapped her fingers on the granite top. "There was an old music box in my closet that I found. It is seriously creepy, Amanda. When I played it yesterday, I blanked out for a couple hours. Twice, I tucked it away in the corner of the closet and twice, something moved it back into my room."

"What? That's crazy. Are you sure?"

Paige rolled her eyes at the ceiling. "Amanda! You need to ask after what just happened upstairs?"

"Okay, okay. But still... I don't get it." Amanda closed her eyes and shook her head from side to side, "If she's a ghost, which I'm still not one hundred percent convinced of...okay, maybe eighty percent convinced...why would she want it and where is it now?"

"I had to get it out of here. It's in my car now." Paige pulled herself higher in the chair, chin tilted high. She opened the laptop to boot it up."

"Just give it to her, Aunt Paige." Julian's voice was followed by Avril's. "Yeah."

"I've got to agree with the kids. Get the bloody thing and put it back where you found it! We can't go through this again. If this is in fact, her way of letting us know she wants it returned. Which of course, I'm—"

"Yeah, yeah. You're not convinced, I get it." Paige clicked on the sites she'd visited earlier. "I'll put it back but I'm not sleeping in that room. Not with that box in there." She looked over at the other three. "And Avril's not going in that room again! Actually, I think we should stay together until we figure this out." Her gaze drifted over to her niece. "I hate that Avril ran upstairs away from us."

"Can I have some brownies?" Julian looked at his mother and then turned to Paige. "It was weird when she passed through me. It felt really cold and I was...I was so *mad*." He looked down at the table and his voice was soft. "I hated you."

Paige could only stare at him, torn between relief that he had woke, was now himself again, and anger at this Cora character.

Her finger tapped the computer screen and spun it so that Amanda could read. She reached across the table and her hand rested on Julian's head. "It wasn't you who hated me. It was her. We're going to find a way of keeping her *away* from us." She rose to her feet and got the brownies from the fridge, setting the plate in the centre of the island.

Amanda was busy reading the site that Paige had earmarked. After a minute or two, she spoke, "We've got sea salt." She blew out a gush of air through pursed lips. "Not sure about any of this...but I can't ignore what just happened in Avril's room."

Paige's cell phone rang and she scooped it out of her pocket. 'Unknown Name' Her eyebrows popped high and she answered quickly. "Matt?" His timing couldn't be better.

# CHAPTER NINETEEN

Paige saw Amanda go to the pantry and take a blue canister of sea salt from the shelf.

She held the phone to her ear, watching her sister pour a line of the coarse granules across the window sill and the doorway.

"Are you sure you don't need me to come over there? I can go through the house to check it." Matt's tone of voice was now worried as opposed to the initial skepticism when she'd told him what had just happened.

"I think we'll be fine. I'll put the music box back in the closet, and tonight we're all going to sleep in the same room. And don't forget we've got the sea salt."

She glanced over at the kids who were busy watching a cartoon on her laptop. They sat quietly, totally immersed in the story, the ghost already a thing of the past.

"What about your sister's husband? Is he coming back early to be with you guys?" Matt sounded irritated now.

She took a deep breath. "He needs to be in Montreal for work this week. There's some kind of thing going on and..." Her voice trailed off.

Josh was going to be the next person she and Amanda had to talk to. That was going to be a hard call, especially since Amanda was still having a difficult time processing all of this.

"Well, call me if you need me, okay? Other than that, I'll meet up with you tomorrow at five. You think you can find the library?"

Paige couldn't help the chuckle that escaped her lips. It actually felt good to laugh. "You mean in the village that consists of four buildings? I think I'll manage."

"Yeah. Okay. Sure."

"I'm really looking forward to meeting your aunt. Thanks Matt, for your offer to help here this evening. See you tomorrow."

"You take care. Bye."

She heard the click of his phone signing off and held hers close to her cheek for a moment. It really was nice of him to offer to help. She took a deep breath and let it out slowly. His aunt would have the story on the house. Maybe there had been some foul play way back when and the spirit was still in the house, angry or confused about leaving. Wasn't that the way these haunted houses things were supposed to go? The ghost needed guidance, a nudge to get them up to heaven or some other plane of existence.

Amanda walked over and placed her hand on Paige's shoulder. "Can you dish out the salad and casserole for the kids? I'm going to call Josh."

Paige rose to her feet and looked up at her sister. "Do you want me to talk to him? What are you going to tell him?"

"Darned if I know. But he'll understand my concern when I tell him Julian fainted." She rolled her eyes and smiled. "He'll probably have some sort of explanation for the doors banging. Actually, I'd like that. It'd be a whole lot better than accepting the haunted house theory."

A half hour later, Amanda turned from looking out the window at the yard. She'd been speaking quietly with Josh and now she held the phone in her hand. "He's upset about Julian. He thinks we should have taken him to the doctor to have him checked out."

"He's fine, Amanda. Look at him."

Julian sat on the floor tossing a yellow rubber ball for Barney to fetch, while his sister laughed and chased after the dog, trying to get it before he did.

You'd never know that anything weird had happened at all. If only it had been some sort of crazy dream. But it wasn't. And the music box was still in the suitcase in the trunk of her car. She sighed and looked over at Amanda again. "Do you think he believed you, Amanda? You did tell him about the door banging on its own and the picture on the wall?"

Amanda slumped down into a chair and her face was tight staring at the floor. "Of course." She slumped, looking over at Paige. "He kind of brushed it off, like it hadn't happened. That's not like Josh. Even if he doesn't believe in any of this paranormal stuff...usually he would still listen to me. He sounded angry."

"Angry? What the hell?" Paige popped up out of her seat and began stacking the dishes in the dishwasher.

"Yeah. I know." Amanda rose to help her, standing at the sink. "Maybe he's run out of patience with me. A depression for over a year and then uprooting everyone to move to a place where we don't know a soul. And then I tell him the house we bought is haunted?" Amanda's voice became low and monotone. "It's a wonder he didn't ask for a divorce."

Paige's gut twisted as she listened to her sister. She knew that tone of voice. She'd lived with it for a year. There was no way she'd let Amanda backslide into depression again. Not now. Not ever. She turned and her hands gripped Amanda's arms. "Josh would never do that, Amanda! He adores you and the kids. He's busy with work. Besides which, he's an engineer— Science is his God. This is way beyond his frame of reference."

Amanda took a deep breath but her shoulders still were slumped low when she nodded at Paige.

Paige's teeth ground together. Dammit Amanda! You can't do this! "We can handle it, Sis! Josh can do his thing, but this house...we've got this covered! Whatever ghost or ghoul thinks they've got a lock on this farm, trying to scare us away...well, they've never dealt with the Bradford sisters. I need you to be strong, Amanda. Julian and Avril need you to be strong."

The intensity of the exchange must have infected the kids as well. Julian and Avril joined Paige and Amanda, putting their arms around the two women's thighs, creating a group hug.

There were tears in Amanda's eyes when she looked down at the two children, nodding and brushing her hand over their heads. She looked over at Paige. "You're right. We will do this. No ghost is going to run us out of town."

Paige laughed. "It's a showdown at the Okay Corral."

"What's an okay corral?" Julian looked up and smiled at her.

"A bad western movie, that's what." She looked over at the window. The light was fading and she still needed to get the music box out of her car and back upstairs. It really was showdown time.

# CHAPTER TWENTY

"All right then." Paige took a deep breath and looked at the others. "We all have to stay together. Got that, Avril?" She looked down and smiled when Avril nodded.

"What about the salt? Should we take it with us?" Amanda's gaze was intent staring at her sister.

"Can't hurt, right?" Paige grabbed her set of car keys from her purse. "C'mon Barney." She led the way out of the kitchen and paused at the doorway. "Careful to step over the line of salt. Try not to disturb it." They had only the one canister of salt and who knew how much would be needed later? They would go into the city and buy whatever other items they needed to cleanse the house and protect themselves...but that wouldn't be until tomorrow.

Everything looked normal in the dining room and foyer when she walked through and stood at the front door. Amanda, holding Avril in her arms and clutching Julian's hand was right at her heels. Paige grimaced before opening the door and stepping out onto the veranda. The air was a bit cooler and the whirring chirp of cicadas filled the night. It was surreal, how everything could be so normal and calm outside, an outright denial of what had happened earlier.

"You stay here and I'll be right back." The car was parked in the driveway about twenty feet away. Her feet crunched the gravel when she walked over, gingerly finding her way in the dim light. She fumbled trying to get the key into the lock at the back of the small car.

The dog started barking and Paige felt her knees turn to water. All of a sudden it felt like eyes were watching her. The key slid into the lock and she shuddered, lifting the lid of the trunk. It was a hole as black as tar that her hand felt around in until her fingers closed on the handle of the overnight bag. Just touching it, knowing that the spooky music box was inside made her skin crawl.

She lifted it out and slammed the lid of the trunk down, breaking the stillness of the night. She raced across the driveway and up and over the veranda. A sigh of relief blew from her lips when she stood inside with the door shut and locked behind her.

"Can I see it?" Amanda leaned forward, peering at the bag.

Julian tugged at the hem of Amanda's shirt. "No Mommy. Let's just put it back. It's Cora's and she wants it."

The fine hair on Paige's neck rose high, when she saw the fear in Julian's eyes. "He's right. Let's get rid of it. She wants it back? She can have it. Just leave us alone."

THUD! THUD!

Paige jumped. She looked to the top of the stairs where the loud banging noise had come from. Her stomach roiled at the thought of going up there...going down the hall to her room. She knew that the thuds had been her bedroom door opening and then slamming shut.

"Mommy!" Avril screamed and buried her face in the curve of Amanda's shoulder. Her hands were white knuckled grasping her mother's shirt.

"Oh my God, Paige! What the hell was that? We can't take the kids up there! Let's get out of here." Amanda gripped Julian's arm, turning to the door.

Julian squirmed out of his mother's grasp. "No Mommy! She'll follow us. We need to put it back where Aunt Paige found it! Cora will leave us alone then." His eyes welled up with tears. "She told me."

Paige's heart wrenched seeing how scared Julian was. He was only a little boy! This shouldn't be happening to him. Her fist clenched on the handle of the bag and she strode towards the stairs. The dog was right beside her. She turned and looked over at Amanda. "Stay here with the kids. I'll deal with this."

When she stomped up the stairs, a picture of the fortune teller's card, the one showing the future with the burning tower and guy falling from it, flashed in her mind. Climbing higher, it was like that. She was walking into danger, the ghost's lair. The fact that Cora had wanted her to claim that bedroom filled her with cold dread.

Her knees felt like they'd turned to rubber, about to give out but she willed herself on. Maybe Julian was right. She'd put the music box back and that would be the end of it. Her door was at the end of the hall, shut tight. Just ten feet away. When she took a few more steps, the door creaked slowly opening. The breath froze in her chest and her hand shook, hearing the high pitched wail of the hinge, an unseen hand moving the door.

The lamp on her bedside table cast an eerie glow over the floor and her chaise lounge. She crept in softly, looking around the room, barely daring to breathe. At movement to her right, her head jerked to the side, and her breath froze in her throat. The closet door inched open.

Paige's heart pounded so hard and fast that she thought it might explode. Still, she continued, her feet whispering softly on the wood, moving steadily towards the closet. She paused and her fingers trembled undoing the belts and then the zippered opening of the bag.

A note of music almost sent her screaming from the room when she picked the box out of the canvas bag. The swirls of inlaid wood that she'd thought were beautiful at first, now looked evil and dark. Carrying the box at chest level, like it was a stick of dynamite instead of the antique it was, she walked into the dark closet. Her feet brushed by her sandals and a pair of leather boots under the rack of clothes.

When her foot bumped into something solid, she let out a breath of air. This was it. She bent and lowered the box, setting it in the corner where she'd found it. Slowly, she backed out, unable to see the box but feeling its malevolence. Her fingers glided along the frame of the door and she turned. The bedroom door was just a few feet away.

She ran across the room and pulled the door shut behind her.

"Paige? Are you okay?" Amanda's voice shot up the stairwell.

She sprinted down the hall, unable to answer her sister right away. She gulped air as she scurried down the stairs. "I'm fine...I think."

Amanda looked up at the ceiling, cocking her head to the side. "It's quiet now. Maybe that did the trick."

Paige looked to Julian for confirmation. He wiped the tears from his eyes and he nodded slightly. Now she could breathe easier. Still...when they all crowded into Amanda and Josh's bedroom later, she'd make sure the light stayed lit all night!

# Chapter Twenty-One

S itting in the overstuffed chair in the master bedroom, Paige looked over to her sister on the bed with the children. Julian and Avril were snuggled together like sleeping Cherubs, next to their mother. The bedside light cast a dim glow, creating dark shadows in the four corners of Amanda's bedroom. At Barney's soft sigh, stretching in front of the door, Paige turned and smiled down at the dog.

"It seems surreal...what happened earlier in Avril's room. If anyone had ever told me I'd be camped out, the four of us sharing a bedroom in a house this big, too frightened to be alone, I'd have said they were on cheap drugs. This is crazy." Amanda whispered before rolling her eyes.

Paige nodded and settled deeper into the plush cushions, tugging the fleece throw higher on her arms. The night was cool like any autumn evening...at least that was what she hoped was affecting the temperature of the room. She wouldn't stake her life on the fact it wasn't just the creepiness of the house. "Maybe tomorrow we'll find out more and hopefully figure out a way to get whatever is here to leave."

Amanda polished off the rest of her wine and smiled. "Either that or we're going to go broke buying salt. I used half a box doing the kitchen and this bedroom. What is it about salt anyway?"

"I don't know, but all the websites say to use it. That and crystals and burning sage..."

Paige looked into Amanda's eyes. It had been years since either one of them had been to church even though they had both gone to Catholic schools, had done all the early sacraments. They had both drifted away as they got older. "What about getting a priest in to bless the house? That's supposed to work."

Amanda stared silently for a few moments. "It feels hypocritical. I think I'd like to leave that as a last resort. If it comes to the point that it's either that or run screaming from the house...well then, for sure we will." Her finger brushed the rim of the glass and her voice became softer. "I wish Josh was here."

Paige sat straighter and took a deep breath. Yeah. Even if he didn't believe in all of this ghostly stuff, at least it would mean another adult in the house. "Did he say when he'll be home?"

"Not until Friday night, if we're lucky. There's a problem at work that they're trying to deal with."

"There's a problem here, we're trying to deal with too!" Paige finished the wine and walked over to the bureau to set the glass down.

At the faint musical notes that sounded, the hair on the back of her neck spiked. She spun around, staring wide eyed at her sister. It was clear from the 'O' her mouth had become, Amanda heard it too. Even Barney raised his head, looking towards the wall.

"Is that what I think it is?" Amanda threw the covers back and scrambled over to stand next to Paige. "How could that be?"

Paige's breath froze in her chest. The hollow, tinny notes of the tune became louder. Oh my God! Cora was in the bedroom down the hall—her bedroom!— making the music box play.

Amanda looked over at the children who still slept soundly, the notes not registering with them at all. But Barney had risen to his feet and the line of fur on his spine, his hackles, spiked high.

There was a soft thud as if a door had swung open and banged against the wall. Footsteps, steady and slow followed. It felt like her eyes would pop out on her cheeks she stared so hard at the door to Amanda's room. The footsteps were coming down the hall outside...closer and closer. Her heart thudded in her chest and she was barely aware of Amanda's fingers digging into her arm.

"Oh my God." Amanda hardly dared to whisper.

There was a rumbling growl and Paige looked down at the dog. Barney's teeth were bared and his eyes were narrow staring at the bedroom door. Whatever it was, had stopped right outside. Oh shit, shit, shit.

She jumped at the thundering bark, and Barney snarling, crouched low before the door.

"Shush!" She grabbed at the dog's collar and tried to pull him back.

"Mommy?" It was Julian's voice.

She'd grabbed the dog too late. It was bad enough that Amanda and she had to go through this nightmare, but now Julian was awake.

She could see the edge of the line of salt peeking out from under the door. She crossed her fingers. It had better work!

The music stopped. The stillness in the room and outside was only broken by the low rumble in Barney's throat and the blood pounding in Paige's ears.

The footsteps started again—this time walking down the hall back to Paige's room. Her bedroom door slammed with a thud that shook the walls. With a yelp, Amanda and Paige rushed over to the bed and huddled close to Julian and Avril. It was over. At least for now.

Sleep was a long time coming for both of the Bradford sisters.

# Chapter Twenty-Two

When Paige woke up the next morning the sunshine streaming through the window pierced her skull in the spot behind her right eye with a dull throbbing ache. Avril sat cross-legged, Indian style next to her, her gap-toothed grin beaming down. Even though she'd only slept for a few hours and those hours had been plagued with nightmares, it was hard to be out of sorts looking into the child's happy face.

She pulled the toddler closer and kissed the top of her head, smelling the fresh baby scent of Avril's skin.

"Aunt Paige?" Julian slid over on the bed, next to her leg.

The shower running in the small bathroom ensuite hissed. Amanda was up already and in there. Paige smiled at Julian. "Good morning."

"Cora is still here. That was her last night." His blue eyes filled with tears and he snuggled closer to her thigh. "I want to go home."

She sat up and folded him in her arms. "This is home, buddy." Pulling back, she lifted his chin and looked into his eyes. "Don't worry. Today I'm going to find out more about Cora or whatever the thing in this house is, that's scaring us. We're going to convince her to leave. Trust me."

"What about the barn? There's something scary in there too." He looked down at the duvet, rolling the soft cotton fabric between his fingers.

Paige took a deep breath. One thing at a time. She turned when the door to the ensuite bath opened and Amanda, already dressed for the day, walked in.

"What's up? You okay Julian?" She whisked the towel from her wet hair and strode over to the bed.

"When's Daddy coming home? Can we go visit him at work?" Julian's lower lip and chin trembled and Avril reached to comfort him.

Amanda's arms went around both children and her gaze was intent meeting Paige's. "Daddy won't be home for another couple of days. Don't worry, kids. Your Aunt Paige and I will make sure nothing bad happens to you. Think of it as an adventure...kind of like an episode of Scooby Doo. There's always a happy ending on that show, right?"

Paige rolled her eyes and sighed. If only it were that simple. But it might work in reassuring Julian, since he loved that cartoon. "Hey! You know how things get really bad for the gang when they split up, Julian? We're not going to make that mistake. We're all staying together today and tonight or at least until we get Cora to leave."

She tapped Julian's shoulder and when he turned to look at her, she pantomimed the crazy dog on Scooby Doo, "Weady for Scoobie snacks? Bweckfast?"

Julian grinned and shook his head. "You don't sound like him, Aunt Paige. He says 'Roobie Racks'."

Amanda looked over at Paige and smiled in unspoken agreement that they'd settled things down for a little while. "We're going to town after breakfast, guys. Maybe we'll have lunch there and go to a park."

Avril bounced on the bed, grinning. "Swings? A slide and jungle gym?"

"For sure!" Amanda swept her daughter up and got to her feet. She looked over at Paige again. "We should go into your room and get your clothes for the day...then Julian's and Avril's."

Paige swallowed hard and pulled the duvet back. Yeah. Going into her room was going to be the spooky one for sure, especially after last night with the music box and footsteps. But it couldn't be helped.

The floor was chilly on her feet and she was glad she had worn a T shirt and a pair of Amanda's flannel pajama bottoms to bed. But there was no way she could borrow jeans or a dress from her sister without it practically falling off her slender frame. Amanda was a few inches taller and at least twenty pounds heavier than Paige.

When she stepped by Barney to get to the door, the dog bounded to its feet, panting and whining a little. Of course. The poor beast had to go outside. She opened the door and looked both ways. Nothing there. Good. She exhaled slowly and stepped out into the hallway. Taking a deep breath she walked to her room. Amanda's footsteps sounded softly behind her, which was some small comfort.

The door was a few inches ajar and she pushed it gently, to open it. She gasped and had to steel herself from jerking back at what she saw in the room. Her clothes were strewn on the floor everywhere, the drawers of her dresser gaping open and empty. The pillowed mattress was bare and the bedclothes lay in a heap under the window. But like the crown jewel, the music box was set on top of the dresser, perfectly centered.

Amanda's shoulder brushed lightly against hers and she gasped. "Holy cow. What happened..."

Paige pulled her shoulders back and her chin tilted high. She strode into the room and began snatching her clothes up from the floor and setting them on the bed. "Listen Cora or whatever your name is...LEAVE MY STUFF ALONE! I PUT YOUR BLOODY MUSIC BOX BACK SO YOU CAN BLOODY WELL LEAVE MY SHIT ALONE! GOT IT?"

She stomped into the closet and huffed a sigh seeing the heap of clothes on the floor amidst the tangle of hangers. There was a blue cotton top and a pair of jeans that she had intended on wearing that day, piled in the corner. She scooped them up, grabbed some underwear and a bra from the pile on the bed and stormed out of the room. She slammed the door shut and forced a tight smile at Amanda and the kids.

"There! Now your room, Julian."

Amanda grinned and led the way holding onto Julian's hand. She turned and a chuckle erupted from her throat before she spoke, "We're going to give your room a double dose of sea salt, Paige. That'll teach whatever or whoever messed up your room a lesson!"

Paige's fingers formed fists so hard that her fingernails cut into the skin in her palms. She breathed slow and deep through flared nostrils following Amanda and Julian. Avril's thumb was once more in her mouth, when she looked over her mother's shoulder at Paige. They had never seen their aunt this angry.

Paige's eyes narrowed watching Amanda gather Julian's clothes. She knew the first stop she'd make that day in town. Before the end of the day, they'd have sage, crystals, holy water and *bags* of salt to deal with this house.

# CHAPTER TWENTY-THREE

W hen Paige trooped into the library in Inveraray at five that afternoon, Matt was lounging in a chair reading a magazine. Paige smiled when he looked up and saw Amanda, Julian and Avril in tow behind her, his eyes opening wide in a double take.

The smell of books filled the air, an ancient dusty scent that filled Paige's nostrils as she strode over to Matt. The library was really just one large room with a door at the back with the word 'Staff' tacked onto it. At the side wall, under a large window was a counter, where an elderly lady in a red top stood, peering at a computer screen from behind glasses perched on the end of her nose.

Paige's stomach did a little summersault looking at Matt's perfect sculpted face and she fell into his dark blue eyes for a moment before recovering herself. "Hi! Found the place!" Paige grinned and turned slightly to include Amanda and the children. "You remember my sister Amanda and her kids, Julian and Avril?"

Matt grinned, showing a set of perfect teeth behind his dark trimmed beard and moustache. He reached for Amanda's hand and shook it. "Hi! Nice to see you again."

"Amanda wants to talk to your aunt as well."

"Yes. I hope it's okay with you. We're kind of travelling en mass today. Maybe the children can find some books and toys to amuse themselves." Amanda looked around for the kids' corner, if there was one. She nodded to Julian, her eyes directing him to the back of the library.

Julian took Avril's hand. "C'mon Avril. There're toys back there."

"Yes! You'll find blocks and Lego and puzzles too! Help yourself!"

At the elderly lady's high-pitched voice, Paige turned to see her amble over. She looked about two hundred years old but was still pretty spry, her grey eyes twinkling behind the thick glasses. Laugh lines bordered her smile.

"Aunt Barbara, this is the girl I told you about, Paige..." His face went blank with question marks in his eyes.

Paige leaned forward and extended her hand. "Paige Bradford, Ms. Hawley." She turned slightly and smiled at her sister. "And this is Amanda Jenkins, my sister and her two kids, Julian and Avril."

The old lady's hand was thin but her grip was firm holding Paige's hand for a beat longer than usual. She had the same intense look in her eyes as her nephew. "Matt told me your family bought the old Larkspur farm."

Paige glanced down at her hand that was still enveloped in both of Barbara Hawley's. "Yes. I guess, if that's what folks around here call it." She pulled her hand back and watched as Amanda's hand was claimed by the elderly woman, as well.

"Pleased to meet you, Ms. Hawley. I gather you're the local historian in Inverary." Amanda glanced quickly at Paige and then smiled at the librarian.

"There's nothing and no one that Aunt Barbara doesn't know in this neck of the woods." Matt smiled over at his aunt and winked.

Barbara raised her hand and tapped her nephew's arm. "Go on with you. You're always buttering me up so I'll remember you in my will." The warm smile she cast on him showed that there was deep affection between them.

"Of course. I want all four of your cats. You know that." Matt laughed, teasing the old lady.

Barbara rolled her eyes and turned to Paige. "This may take a while to tell you about the farm. Would you like a cup of tea or coffee?" Her hand swept over the sofa and two chairs that were centered in the open area of the room. "Have a seat."

"Nothing for me, thanks. We just had coffee and snacks in town." Paige stepped over to the worn leather sofa and took a seat next to Amanda. She watched Matt and his aunt sit down in the two chairs opposite. The old lady was friendlier than she had expected given Matt's first description—that she was pretty closed mouthed about the farm.

Barbara turned and smiled at her nephew. "Would you mind, dear? I'd love a cup of tea. The tea bags are in the cupboard." Paige could feel the blood rush to her neck and blossom on her cheeks. Busted, checking out Matt's tush. The old lady didn't miss a trick.

Still smiling, Barbara said, "He was almost married a year ago but they called it off at the last minute. It was fine by me. Eleanor was too snobby by half, in my opinion." She leaned back into her chair, her mouth twitching. "I hope he finds the right girl soon."

"Uhhh..." Paige remained tongue tied until Barbara patted her hand.

Amanda sat forward on the edge of her chair. "Ms. Hawley?"

"Please. Most people just call me Barbara." The smile dropped from her face and she took a long deep breath. "Normally I don't talk about the Larkspur farm. It would be like gossip and I don't waste my time with that. But you bought the place, so it's not gossip, is it? You need to know about it or you wouldn't be here, right?"

"Yes. There's been a few things that have happened since we arrived." Amanda glanced over at Paige and sighed.

"My sister is, or rather *was* a skeptic," Paige said. "But whatever is in that house knocked her son unconscious yesterday. He's fine now. Just scared, like the rest of us." Paige's fingers had been clasped tight together on her lap but when she saw Barbara nod slowly, the look of concern in her eyes, she relaxed a bit.

"I see," Barbara said. "Larkspur's a..." after a pause, she set her lips. "It's a different sort of place, isn't it?"

Paige felt a sense of relief wash over her. At least she didn't have to spend a lot of time convincing Barbara. It was obvious she knew things about the house. "That's putting it mildly," she said.

Nodding, Barbara looked up at the ceiling. "The first tragedy that I know of... to strike at Larkspur was back in the 1930's. Elmer Larkspur was twenty-one when he inherited the house from his grandparents. He lived there with his wife and two children before he..." Barbara looked down at her lap, and sighed. "...he went crazy one night. He shot his wife and his youngest child before going into the barn and killing himself. Blew his head off."

Barbara turned at the sound of the staff door opening. She continued talking, watching Matt enter the room again. "The oldest boy was visiting his aunt on his mother's side. That's what saved him that horrible night."

Amanda's fingers closed around hers and squeezed them tight, never letting go, even when Matt appeared carrying a mug of steaming tea for his aunt. The elderly woman smiled at him and then took a sip of tea. The clunk of the mug being set on the table was the only sound in the large room.

"How could someone do that? Was he sick? Mentally ill or something?" Amanda shook her head and then turned, looking for the kids who were sitting at a small table at the back of the room.

Barbara's eyes were sad and a grimace formed on her lips. "My father thought so. They were kids in school together. Elmer was always a loner. People thought he was shy but maybe there was more to it than that. That year was a bad year for farmers. There was a drought and then beetles ate what crop managed to survive. Dad thought that the financial strain on the farm was the final straw for Elmer."

Paige's mouth slowly gaped open as she listened to the old woman. Her heart beat faster and she strained closer to the edge of the chair. Oh my God. A family murdered. A little kid. And a suicide! "He killed himself in the barn," she said quietly. "That barn is very weird."

Barbara nodded. "Yes. It's an odd building, isn't it? When I was a child a gang of us went out to the farm on a dare. It was the 1950's and the place had been abandoned for years. But unlike other abandoned farms, it had been untouched..." her voice faded as she looked off into space, back to her yesterdays.

"Looks more like a church than a barn if you ask me," Paige said. She shook her head. "But what do I know? I'm a girl from the big city."

Barbara turned her gaze to Paige. "A chapel? That's what we all thought when we went out there." She looked away again. "We only went the one time. None of us had the gall to break into the farmhouse, but we went down the path to the barn." She shook her head and gave a half smile. "From the moment we stepped onto the path, I wanted to leave."

"Why?"

"It just felt... *wrong.*"

"Wrong?" said Matt. "You were just a bunch of kids snooping around an abandoned place." He shrugged his shoulders. "No big deal."

Barbara shook her head. "No, I didn't feel guilty, Matt. I felt afraid. It was the place. It was wrong." She turned her head, taking in the gazes of her guests. "All the children felt it that day. Only one of us went into the barn, actually."

"The door was wide open, I'll bet," said Paige.

Barbara nodded. "But the closer we got, the funnier we felt. Dennis Piazetski was the only one brave enough to go inside... but he only got halfway across the barn floor when he stopped and threw up." Barbara's voice grew quiet. "It was a beautiful warm summer's day, but I can still remember the chills I felt out there. After Dennis threw up, we got out of there as fast as we could." She sat back in her chair. "None of us kids—and there had to be at least six of us—ever spoke of that afternoon again." She shivered. "I got curious about the place though and asked my father about it, him being a friend of Elmer and all." Her eyes brightened. "He told me something very strange."

"What?" Paige leaned in.

"He told me that barn is cursed somehow."

"Cursed?" Amanda asked. "That's crazy."

"No, there's something about that building. My father said that Elmer built it himself, by hand, one board at a time. And the further along he got, the more peculiar he became. It was very hard times back then, especially for farmers. The depression was in full swing, and the winds of war were stirring in Europe. But still, instead of getting a job to make some money, Elmer spent every waking hour of the last year of his life building that barn."

The room was silent as Barbara continued her tale. "He came into town on the last day. My father owned a hardware store on Princess Street and Elmer came in to buy shells for his shotgun. Papa said the man looked like he hadn't had a bath in a month. His hair was greasy and needed a trim and he smelled to high heaven." She dropped her head, remembering every word her father had said. "Lord knows, he needed a shave. His clothes were a wreck; his work jacket was torn in several places and his trousers had holes in the knees."

Lifting her head, she continued. "Papa told me that he tried to talk about the hunting in Elmer's area, but Elmer only said that his barn was finished and now the war could begin."

"The war?"

"Yes." Barbara turned to lift her mug of tea, but her hand shook. She let it back down and turned back to the group. "He came into my father's store on the afternoon of September 2nd, 1939."

"You can remember the date?" Matt asked with a weak smile.

"No, silly. My father told me. My father remembered the date exactly. You see, that night, Elmer slaughtered his family... and the next day England declared war on Germany and the Second World War began."

As one, Amanda, Paige and Matt all gasped.

Barbara leaned forward to Amanda. "That barn needs to be destroyed."

Amanda laughed. "My husband wouldn't dream of it! It's going to become the workshop he always wanted." Setting her mouth, she added, "And I'm going to board animals there too."

Paige glanced over at Matt. Their eyes met and there was a frown on his face before his hand rose to rub the back of his neck. She turned to Barbara, "So what happened to the son and the farm after that?"

"Jack Larkspur. That was the son. Of course, he inherited the farm but he wanted no part of it. Instead, he moved in with his aunt. Back then, we didn't know so much about mental illness. The murder and Jack's suicide...it was not only a tragedy; it was a scandal. The aunt and her family moved away...down to the States. The house sat empty for a long, long time."

Paige's eyes narrowed. "But the ghost we encountered was a girl. At least that's what Julian sensed. Avril said she saw her. There's also a music box..."

Barbara picked up the mug of tea and took a long, loud sip. "Ah yes. Cora Slipp. Or as the kids at school used to call her, Cora Slut. She was my student in grades seven and eight. They didn't think I knew, but of course I did." She sighed. "Poor Cora."

"Wait a minute. What happened to the house? Who bought it?" Amanda interrupted, straining forward.

Barbara's head jerked back. "Yes. Of course. You must think I'm doddering to leave that part out."

Matt guffawed. "Yeah right. No one could ever accuse you of that, Aunt Barbara."

She tapped her nephew's knee and grinned. "Keep that up and you'll have a house full of cats in no time. Actually, I think Whiskers is quite fond of you already." She cleared her throat and looked across at Amanda. "It was 1966 when the house finally sold to the Slipp family. As I said they were there for two years before Cora's break-down."

"Her breakdown? How did she die? She did, didn't she?" Paige could tell from the tone of Barbara's voice when she said 'breakdown' that it had ended tragically for Cora. Not that she had any great sympathy for the girl ghost who had knocked Julian out and scared the life out of all of them!

Barbara was silent for a few moments holding her mug of tea and looking down at her lap. "It was horrible what happened to that girl and her family. She was the younger child. She had a brother Sean who was a few years older. Her mother and father were terribly religious and very strict with her. Even the way she dressed, always a skirt that hung below her knees in an era when hemlines were rising. There was a model in England - Twiggy— she made the mini skirt all the rage. But poor Cora was boy crazy. She'd hike her skirt, rolling the waistband, sashaying around and chasing the older boys."

"A girl after my own heart." Matt started to laugh but stopped short at the scowl Barbara shot him. "Sorry."

She sniffed holding her nose high and then continued. "One boy...Greg Armitage liked her. He started hanging around her and bringing her little presents. Flowers, candy—"

"A music box?" Paige's eyes were wide as saucers. She pictured the young girl in the green dress dancing to its tune.

Barbara's forehead furrowed even deeper and her head tilted to the side. "Why yes. Now that you mention it, I seem to recall a music box...it was beautiful...it had inlaid wood." She took a deep breath and looked over at Paige. "Greg's parents were well off. His father had a restaurant and tavern in the city. Of course, something like that would have completely incensed Roy Slipp and his wife. They were church-goers—all day Sunday and twice during the week. They had real problems with the evil of alcohol."

The old lady took a deep breath and shook her head. "The school year was beginning to wind down; it was early June. Greg was in the eighth grade and Cora was in the seventh. He wanted her to come to his graduation dance at the end of the school year." Her eyes became teary. "Her parents must have found out or something. She was cruelly beaten by them."

"What?" Amanda and Paige asked. "What happened?"

Barbara hung her head. "Things were different in those days." Her head still down, she said, "I was doing all I could, but it wasn't enough." She lifted her head again. "Cora died the week before the dance. It was the next day we heard about the deaths. Again, all of them killed. Cora did it. Stabbed them with a carving knife. Then she killed herself in the barn."

"Oh my God." Amanda's words were little more than a breath of air. She sat back and closed her eyes for a moment.

Paige rubbed her hand on her sister's arm. "It's okay, Amanda. At least now we know what we're dealing with."

"Do you? Do you really know?" Barbara set the mug on the table and got up. She strode over to the counter and pulled a worn, red scrapbook from a shelf behind it. She handed the book to Paige. "I suggest you read this. There's more at work here than just mental illness and a haunting."

Paige opened the book and leafed through a few pages. It was filled with old newspaper clippings and photocopied articles. Most were headlined with historical events—the Second World War, the assassination of Martin Luther King and Bobby Kennedy. She peered at Barbara; her eyes narrow with question marks. "What does this mean?"

"Kennedy was murdered the same night that Cora's family died."

"You're saying there's a connection?"

"I'm saying that the horrible things that happened on Larkspur Lane took place just before horrible things happened in the world."

"Like a blasting cap, Aunt Barbara?" Matt said.

The three women turned to Matt with confusion in their eyes.

"Look, if you want to blow up a stick of dynamite, you don't just light a fuse and boom. The fuse ignites the blasting cap, and then you get the ka-boom. A smaller bang makes the big bang possible." He held out his hands. "Like priming a pump?"

"Oh," said Barbara. "I can understand priming a pump." She turned to Amanda. "Are you sure you want to live in that house? After all you've heard?"

Paige turned and looked at her sister. This was Amanda's call ultimately. She saw the look of defiance burn in Amanda's narrow eyes and she smiled. Yeah. Paige wasn't the only one with a fierce temper once it was riled.

"It's *our* house now." Amanda's chin rose and she sat straighter.

The old lady's gaze became sharper still, never leaving Amanda's. "You will need the gifts of your son and your sister. If not for them, I would advise you to move back to Toronto."

Paige's lips fell open watching Barbara. The only way she could have known that Julian and she were 'gifted' was if the old lady shared the same sixth sense. The fact that she acknowledged the gift, and actually felt it was the only way of dealing with the supernatural entities in the Larkspur homestead, was oddly comforting.

Barbara looked over at her nephew and nodded slowly before turning to Paige. "We will work at cleansing the house and barn of spiritual entities, but first things first...we need to figure out a way to protect you and your family."

'*Protection*.' The old fortune teller's warning and a flash of the tower, with the lightning bolt and the person falling appeared in Paige's mind and she shuddered.

Julian wandered over from the children's section and stood next to her, placing his hand on her knee as he stared at the old lady. "Help us...please."

# CHAPTER TWENTY-FOUR

When Barbara leaned forward, resting her hand on Julian's shoulder, the small silver cross tucked inside her blouse slipped out, glinting in the library's low lighting. "I will help you. I promise."

Paige took a deep breath and felt the knot of muscle in the back of her neck let go. The cross and the kind wisdom of Matt's aunt was reassuring. "We bought sage, crystals and a ton of salt today. Is there anything else you think we need to do tonight?"

Matt got up and picked the mug from the table, his eyes darting from Paige to Barbara. "Surely, you're not going to go out there tonight and start all this? Stay the night in a hotel and tackle this in the morning. I'd say you probably need a good night's sleep anyway."

He took a few steps, on his way to the staff room but stopped abruptly, peering at his aunt. "Is it enough, do you think? If all of this is true and the place is haunted, we'll need more than salt and herbs to fix this...just saying."

A slow smile twitched at the corners of Paige's lips. Matt had definitely included himself in the group. This was even more reassuring or maybe it was misery loving company. She wasn't sure which. She grinned at him. "Don't forget the crystals, we got those too, you know."

He threw a quick glare her way and then shook his head continuing on to the staff room.

"He's right, I'm afraid. We do need more. But we need to start this tonight. On that score he's wrong." Barbara stood up and smiled seeing Avril skip over from the library's play area. "Hi honey."

"So, you're coming out to the house with us?" Amanda stood and swung Avril up into her arms. She turned to Paige, "Poor Barney. He's probably bursting. I'd better go out and let him out of the jeep." She smiled at

Barbara, and extended her hand. "Thank you so much! Of course, you'll have dinner with us."

Barbara's hands closed over Amanda's. "A piece of toast and a cup of tea is all I need." She winked at Avril. "Although that thumb looks pretty good too."

Immediately Avril's hand dropped from her lips and she hid her face in Amanda's neck.

When Amanda smiled and walked across the room and out the door, Barbara brushed her hand over Julian's head. "You're a brave little boy, aren't you?"

He reached for Paige's hand and then nodded at the old woman. She gave it a gentle squeeze, feeling her chest warm with love for the little boy. He shouldn't have to go through this...and he'd been the one knocked unconscious.

When the door to the staff room opened and Matt appeared, Paige smiled at the confused look in his eyes. "You're invited for supper. We're all going out to the house. Larkspur." She looked down at Julian. "That's the name of a flower, did you know that?"

"What? We're doing this *tonight*?" Matt frowned at his aunt.

"Enough, young man. You can at least remember your manners and thank the young lady for her offer of dinner." She clucked her lips and then strode over to the counter. "I need to stop at my house to pick up some things and make sure the cats are fed." Plucking her wool sweater from the back of the chair, she murmured. "God only knows how long I'll be out there."

She strode over with a firm step that belied her many years. "I'll drive with you, Matt." She placed her hand on Paige's arm. "We'll see you out there. My Lord. It's been years since I was out that way."

Paige walked Julian over to the door ahead of Matt and his aunt. When she stepped outside, Amanda was just getting Barney settled in the back of the jeep. The sun was low in the sky and nightfall would be on them in an hour or so. She wondered if perhaps Matt might not have been right in delaying this until the next day.

When they drove up to the limestone home, Paige noticed Amanda peering up at the windows before turning the key and shutting the car's engine off. The setting sun smeared a palette of pink and orange on the glass and stone walls. The door was shut tight and the stained-glass panels bordering it glinted, catching the light and gleaming blood red.

Paige's neck muscles bunched tight when she examined the windows and door. It was a feeling rather than anything concrete that made her heart beat faster. She blew out a fast sigh. "Everything looks the same. But we'll have to see inside. After what happened to my room last night, I'm expecting the worst." She opened the car door and then got Avril out of her car seat and set her on the ground.

"Should we wait for Barbara and Matt before going inside?" Amanda's eyes were round orbs looking at the house, and holding Julian's hand.

Paige shook her head, opening the hatch to let Barney out. "We've got the supplies. Let's get started." She reached for the bags containing the salt, crystals and sage, just as Amanda's cell phone rang.

When she glanced over at her sister, Amanda mouthed the word "Josh" and turned to wander to the edge of the driveway, speaking on the phone all the while.

Paige forced a smile looking at the two kids. It was odd that despite the wide-eyed nervous look in Avril's eyes, her thumb was not in her mouth. That was progress. "Let's go, guys. Hang onto Barney's collar Julian and you guys stay behind me, okay?" She strode up the two stairs and across the veranda.

When she unlocked the door, she noticed the line of salt was thin and scattered. It could be a breeze or draft coming in under the door, but she didn't think so. Her eyes darted over to the stairs and into the open archway of the living room. The only movement showing was flittering dust motes caught in the beam of light shining in through the window. It was quiet. Maybe too quiet. The hair on her arms rose high above the goose bumps.

The kids and dog were right on her heels, creeping across the dining room and into the kitchen. Again, the line of salt was a fraction of what it had been in the morning—as if it had been attacked.

"Aunt Paige?" Julian whispered.

She set the supplies on the island counter and then squatted down, looking into his eyes. "I know. I feel it too. Cora. She's very angry. Is that it?" A feeling like ants skittering up her spine filled her. And for the first time the kitchen actually felt cold.

Even Barney felt it, from the way his fur bristled. The kitchen had always been kind of a safe haven but now...not so much.

Damn. Where were Amanda and Barbara when she needed them?

She took a deep breath and stood up. She popped the spout of the box of salt and handed it to Julian. "You take this and pour a new line across the doorway. I'm going to light the sage bundle." She fished in the bag for the lighter and bundle of dried sage and set them on the counter. Turning to Avril, she lifted her onto the chair. "You stay put, okay?"

The little girl's eyes were wide and tears began to form in them. The thumb plopped into her mouth and she began to suck it with renewed vigor. Paige sighed, picked up her items, and then plucked a large bowl from the kitchen cabinet. She struck the tab on the lighter, setting the bundle of dried herbs alight.

The smell was acrid, and wispy trails of smoke drifted up from the burning embers. She held it over the bowl to catch any stray ashes, and followed Julian to the doorway. "Okay Julian? You'll be fine." Her stomach roiled and her hand shook slightly as she waved the burning bundle. She just wished she felt fine and that this would work.

Julian held the canister in both hands, bending and watching the line of white crystals fall onto the floor. When he finished, he straightened up and there was a small smile on his lips. "It feels a little better already, Aunt Paige."

The front door banged open and footsteps thudded quickly across the dining room. Amanda burst into the kitchen and stood, holding her hands on each side of her face. "Oh God, Paige! Josh is in trouble at work! The company he hired to supply the asphalt for that big project screwed up! They used recycled oil in the mix. The pavement is ruined and everything has to be re-done!"

"So? How is that his fault?"

"He's the guy in charge of quality control! It *was* his fault!"

Paige's mouth fell open and her stomach felt like someone had sucker punched her. "Oh my God. Did they fire him?"

Amanda took a deep breath and now her fingers fisted in her hair. "Not yet. He barely convinced his boss to give him another chance. He's not going to be home for another week. Oh my God, what if he loses this job? We're sunk. All our money is tied up in this place and from the sounds of it, we'll never be able to sell it—not the way it is!"

She sank down onto the stool and tears rolled down her cheeks. "Even last night...when we were so scared. I thought we'd be okay. If worse came to worst we could move back to Toronto, rent an apartment or something and just let this place sit. But if he loses his job, we can't carry two places! We're trapped here!" Her shoulders racked with sobs and she covered her face with her hands. "What a fool I was. Thinking it would be a new start, my dream home! It's a disaster!"

Now Avril was openly crying as well, slipping off the stool and clambering over to her mother.

Paige blinked a few times feeling suddenly dizzy. It was such an unreal nightmare...first the feeling of dread coming into the house...and now knowing that her sister and her family were indeed trapped here if Josh couldn't make amends with the situation at work.

When she looked over at Amanda, the tears streaming down her cheeks and the slumped shoulders, Paige's heart broke. She walked slowly over to her. "We'll fix this, Sis. That's why Barbara and Matt are coming over here. We're all going to fix this."

She set the bowl and sage on the counter and hugged her sister. "This is a setback. But Josh will be okay. They won't fire him. It was the contractor's fault. They'll see that. Have faith. We need you, okay?" Her eyes welled with tears holding her sister who was still sobbing softly. How much could one person endure before they went stark raving mad?

She looked around at the kitchen...at Julian standing with slumped shoulders, on the verge of tears...at the very walls of the house where two families had died. How much had Cora taken before she snapped and killed everyone?

Amanda sat crying, ignoring the small hands that tugged on her shirt...lost in a world of desperation.

Her blood ran cold at her next thought. *How much could Amanda take?*

# CHAPTER TWENTY-FIVE

A t the soft thud of the front door closing, Paige spun around facing the dining room. Her heartbeat spiked for a moment before she heard Barbara's voice calling out from the front of the house.

"Hello?"

When Paige sprinted across the room, she felt the knot in her neck loosen, seeing Barbara and Matt. A large floral tapestry bag hung from the old woman's forearm while her fingers clutched a thick, dark book. The smile fell from her lips and her gaze flickered past Paige into the kitchen. She handed the bag to Matt and stepped quickly past Paige.

Matt's eyes locked with hers. "What's wrong? I mean aside from the obvious." His hand rose and rested lightly on her shoulder, his eyes dark and intent looking at her.

The concerned look and his kindness threatened to turn her inner resolve into a molten puddle of tears. She couldn't do that—not yet. Taking a deep breath, she squared her shoulders. "It's Josh, Amanda's husband. There's a problem at work that we just learned about. He might lose his job."

His eyes closed slowly and he shook his head. "Ah shit. You guys don't need that. Not right now." He pulled her in to his chest and rubbed her back. Without a thought, she wrapped her arms around his waist and they stood in silence for a moment.

Her eyes opened wide in surprise at how much a comfort it was to be in his arms. So soon? She stiffened a little.

Matt sensed it or something, because he put his hands on her shoulders and when she looked up said, "C'mon. Let's go see what we can do to help."

When they entered the kitchen Barbara was handing a glass of water to Amanda. Julian and Avril stood next to their mother, looking up at the old woman.

"Everything will work out, dear. Drink this and try not to worry. It's hard but remember, the darkest hour is just before dawn." Barbara's head turned and she nodded for Paige and Matt to join them. "Matt, I'd like you to stay in the kitchen with Amanda and Avril." When Barney stepped over and nuzzled her hand, she smiled down at him. "And of course, you stay here too. Good boy."

Her gaze turned to Paige and Julian and her eyebrows rose high. "I see you started without me."

"I poured the salt. Is it gonna work?" Julian's chin dropped and he looked down at the floor.

"Have faith, dear." Barbara rustled his curls with her bony hand and looked over at Paige. Her grey eyes never wavered and Paige felt calming strength emanate from the old woman. Barbara had taken control, settling Amanda and getting things underway—years of teaching, taking charge, still showed through.

She looked down at Julian and lifted his chin with her finger. "Since you did such a good job with that, why don't you continue? You're a brave boy."

She took the tapestry bag from Matt and rummaged in it, "Paige, you'll look after the sage smudge." She pulled out one quart glass jar which had a cross etched on the side. "Here we go! The Holy Water."

Paige looked at the sage in her hand and back to Barbara. "Holy Water?" When Barbara nodded, she said, "We're not a religious family. It's okay to burn sage and use Holy Water at the same time?"

Barbara nodded.

"Don't worry, Paige," Matt said with a grin. "Aunt Barb's religious enough for *all* of us." He bobbed his eyebrows at his aunt. "Isn't that right? Even if you don't go to Mass that much anymore?" When Barbara just smiled, he continued. "She was in a convent for a while back in the early '60's."

Paige's jaw dropped. "Like for nuns?" When she saw Barbara nod, she asked, "Why'd you leave? Did you lose your faith or something?"

Barbara dropped her gaze. "No. Not at all." Raising her head, she looked between Paige and Matt. "I fell in love."

"What!" Matt said. "This is news to me! Who? What happened?"

"The who isn't important; he's long since passed away." Her eyes blurred with tears. "He was in the Seminary. We were the dearest of friends, and when it began to…" her voice faltered and she waved her hands. "At any rate, he made his decision, and transferred far away." She looked to Paige.

"My faith? It's never been stronger, dear. But..." she held up a finger. "I've learned in my life that the Universe and the mind of God are far too vast for one faith to hold all its truths." She gestured at the salt, the sage and to her jar of Holy Water. "We'll take our Blessings where we can, and trust."

The room was silent until Amanda stood up. "I don't want Julian doing anything with this. He was knocked unconscious yesterday. He's just a boy..." She looked to each of the others. "I'll take his place." She reached for the canister of salt that was on the counter.

Barbara's hand shot out and gripped Amanda's arm. "No. I'm sorry but in this, he's the stronger one. You need to stay here, where it's peaceful."

BOOM!

The loud noise came from the upstairs above them. It banged again, hard enough to shake the walls. Paige froze. Her heart raced and she felt like she was going to be sick. There was no doubt that the noise had come from her bedroom.

"Holy shit." The pupils of Matt's dark eyes were rimmed with white staring at the ceiling above him. "That's her, right?" His voice was barely above a whisper. He turned to his aunt. "You can't do this Aunt Barbara. What if you get hurt or..."

She smiled. "Then you'll be the proud owner of four cats, won't you?"

"Seriously, Aunt Barb. Tell me what to do and I'll do it. I'm young and strong."

"Yes. But I'm wise." She patted his arm and then turned to Paige. "I'll lead the way. We must go into every room. I will bless the walls with the holy water while you wave the smudge." She looked down at Julian. "You will pour the salt along the door opening when I tell you." Her gaze shot from Paige and then back to Julian. "We're clear?"

Julian nodded while Amanda squeezed his shoulder and bent to kiss his cheek. "Stay close to Paige, Babe." Her eyes were filled with tears when she turned to pick up Avril.

Paige took a fresh bundle of dried sage from the package. There was a tremble in her hands when she lit the coarse sticks and leaves and blew the flame out, watching the embers glow hot orange. She took a deep breath, willing her heart to slow. Oh God. She had to be strong.

BOOM!

Her chest clamped tight. She peered up at the ceiling. Cora didn't like what was about to happen.

# Chapter Twenty-Six

## *November, 1968*

Cora Slipp floated onto the school bus after the best day she'd ever had. As she glided down the aisle between the rows of seats, she could feel the other kids' eyes on her. The word had gotten around about how Greg Armitrage (*her* Greg, thank you very much) had held her hand during lunch hour. The coolest guy in the eighth grade had made her—Cora Slipp, seventh grade loser—*his girlfriend*!

She held her book bag to her chest as she navigated her way down the bus. She didn't want to take a chance and break the treasure Gregg had given her at the end of the day. It was buried in the bottom of her bag and she didn't want to bump it.

She took a seat by herself and went beside the window to wave at Greg. He lived in town and took a different bus. He was standing there, handsome as James Bond waving at her. When he blew her a kiss, she heard three of the girls on the bus all go 'Awww...' at once.

As soon as the bus pulled out, she opened the front pocket of her book bag and took out the package of Kleenex. She had to make sure that she got her eye makeup and lipstick off before the bus did the high school pickup. If Sean caught her, he'd fink her out to Mother in a flash. And enjoy every minute of her troubles.

She had everything off by the time the bus pulled into the high school.

Sean came aboard with the other five high school kids who took that bus out to the countryside. They made eye contact as soon as he got on board, and as usual, his face took on a disdainful expression. Before coming down the aisle, one of the kids from her school grabbed his arm and whispered in his ear. His head shot up and the scornful expression morphed into outright contempt. He flopped into a vacant seat across from her.

"So, Cora Slut, I hear you got a boyfriend," he said with a sneer.

"Shut up!"

He leaned across to her. "Look at you. You have your skirt rolled up almost to your butt." He shook his head slowly and sat back on his seat. "What a mini-skirted slut. Mother is going to be sooo interested."

Oh no! She was so distracted by Greg's gift and the makeup she forgot to roll her skirt back down! Her face flamed red and she dropped her chin, hiding behind the lank of hair that fell forward. There was no point in begging Sean to keep his mouth shut. He'd hated her all her life, and was going to relish the trouble he was going to get her in.

Cora stepped down from the school bus into another world. She scowled watching her brother race ahead, down the long dirt driveway. It was like Cinderella leaving the ball and coming home to drudgery. But it wasn't just the chores—she could do them standing on her head and spitting nickels. No, it was the constant criticism. Anything she did or said, if it didn't have to do with the church then it was the work of the devil.

She stepped in behind the tall spruce tree and slipped her book bag off her shoulder setting it gently on the ground beside her. Her fingers curled under the light white sweater and rolled the waistband of her skirt. She tugged at the fabric covering her hips until the hemline dropped back down, well below her knees. There! Now her mother couldn't say anything.

She peeked inside the book bag, lifting the gym shorts away from the inlaid wooden box. A slow smile spread on her cheeks and her heart floated in her chest. Greg Armitage. He did love her. Why else would he give her such a romantic gift! She would listen to it when she went to bed and dream of the time when they'd be married! Her eyes closed and she almost squealed remembering the feel of his lips on hers at recess, the two of them sitting behind the oak tree out of sight from the rest of the kids.

"Cora!" Her mother's high-pitched yell from the front door of the house broke the spell.

The twelve-year-old girl huffed a sigh. Back to reality, such as it was. "Coming!" She stepped out from behind the tree, sliding the strap of the bag over her shoulder.

Walking up the driveway she felt the dread descend. Thank goodness it was a full moon tomorrow night. She'd show off her treasure to her Mr. Pooka. Since she was little, anything good that happened at school pleased him. And what was in the bottom of her book bag was the grooviest thing ever!

Uh oh. Mother was waiting on the veranda for her, arms akimbo, fists buried in her waist. Sean had scrambled ahead of her to get to the house first, and from the look on her face he wasted no time blabbing. The thin line of her lips told Cora that she was in for it.

Again. She sighed inwardly. She wasn't afraid anymore, just weary of the woman. Nothing ever pleased Mother. Nor Father. Unless it had to do with Sean. Her older brother was the apple of her parents' eye and she was reminded of that every darn day.

Mother's gray eyes were chips of limestone as she stared silently while Cora climbed the few steps to the veranda. Her severity was completed by the tight bun of hair that was knotted tightly at the back of her head. Cora noticed for the first time the woman was going gray.

"Cora Slipp, I'm ashamed of you."

What now? What was it going to be this time? She ran through a check-list in her head. No, she made sure the dishes from breakfast had been dried and put away. Oh no! Did she get all the silverware? She stopped before the woman. "What did I do, Mother?" She already knew the answer. Thanks, big brother. He really *did* hate her.

Mother's hand lashed out and hooked onto the waistband of her skirt and pulled the girl to her. "Ah-ha!" she said as she eyed the top of Cora's skirt. "Look at these creases that go all the way around!" As the girl stood there, her mother began folding them over, her eyes peering down at Cora's hemline as it rose higher and higher. "You're such a little tramp!" she said when Cora's hem was well above her knees. "Such a disgusting, loathsome tramp." Shaking her head slowly, she said in her fake, sad voice, "Your brother told me you had your skirt too high when he got on the bus. I told him he must be wrong. 'What pure Christian girl would do such a thing, Sean?' I said to him."

"All the girls do it, Mother!"

Mother's eyes widened in shock. "They *do it*?" she said, her voice almost a whisper. She eyed Cora up and down. "To attract boys, you disgusting wretch!"

Cora's chin trembled as she stood silently.

She released the girl from her grip and pointed to the lilac bushes with her chin. "Go bring me a switch, Cora."

"Mother! No! I'm sorry! Not the switch! I've been so good!"

"Now. Before I bring your father from the barn."

Oh no. Father would use his belt. Silently, she turned and walked to the lilac bushes. She knew from long and painful experience that if she picked one too green, Mother would summon Father. She would also summon him if she picked out one too thin. She found one that she knew would suit Mother's purpose and with trembling hands broke off a length longer than her forearm. She stood with her back to her mother as tears of fear and anger flowed while she stripped off the leaves. With a sigh more forlorn and resigned than fearful now, she returned to the veranda.

"Cora, I don't do this for pleasure," Mother lied as she took it in hand. Her eyes glimmered as she held it up for examination. "I do this for your own good. Spare the rod..." she shot Cora a look.

With an practiced adroitness borne of repetition, Cora bowed her head and said softly "... spoil the child, Mother."

"Turn away and lean against the porch railing."

Her skirt was still hiked up. She knew what was coming, and she knew it was gonna hurt a LOT. Even so, the searing agony of the first blow was an excruciating strip of pain across both of her thighs. She yelped.

Taking a deep breath, Mother said, "You want to show off your legs to boys, eh?" She leaned into the next lash, the second stroke crossing the first to create a red X on the back of the girl's leg.

Cora was able to keep her mouth closed until Mother went to work on her other leg, repeated lashes building into a crescendo of torment until a shriek, followed by a series of wails exploded out from the girl. The last two searing strokes cut into the delicate skin behind her knees and she collapsed to the floor, crying in pain.

"There!" said Mother, snapping the switch in half and tossing it over the porch railing. "Go to your room and stay there! Pray for forgiveness, and I'll see you in the morning." She turned to the door. "I'll have to manage on my own preparing supper for the family," she said with a tired voice.

At school the next day, she kept to herself. Her legs were aflame, the angry welts covered up by her longest skirt and knee highs. When Greg Armitrage approached her during recess, she flinched when he sat beside her.

"Cora, what's wrong?" he asked. His eyebrows formed a straight line of worry over his deep-set brown eyes.

"Nothing!" she hissed at him. "Just leave me alone!" It broke her heart to say the words, but Mother told her that if she was caught out doing *anything* with boys, Father's wrath would make yesterday's punishment seem like a nice, warm bath.

Jumping up in tears she fled back inside to her classroom. She went to her desk at the back of the room, dropped her head and sobbed.

"Cora, what's the matter?" Oh no! Miss Hawley was at the door to the classroom holding a stack of books. Leaving them at the front, she hurried down the row to Cora. She put her arm across the child's back. "What happened?"

"I... I can't tell you," she sobbed into the crook of her arms. "We never tell."

"Was it Greg Armitrage?" When Cora's head whipped up, Miss Hawley gave a small laugh. "It's alright, dear, I know he's very sweet on you." She paused. "Did he do something bad?"

"No! He's the nicest person ever! I love him!" She scrabbled in her book bag and fished out the music box and opened it. When the tune began to play, she looked up to Miss Hawley. "He gave me this! It's the nicest thing I've ever had!" The tears flowed again, and Cora began to hiccup.

Miss Hawley squatted down beside the girl, admiring the music box. She opened the lid and it began to play.

"I've never heard that tune before, Cora," she said.

"Really? I know that song by heart." Cora's face which had been so full of sadness lightened. "It's my favorite song in the whole world."

"Really? What song is that?"

"I don't know its name, but I can sing it." She closed her eyes and began to sing in a clear voice:

> *Come away with me*
> *We'll always be*
> *Just me and you*
> *Just us two...*
> *When things go bad*
> *And make you sad*
> *Fear not my dear*
> *I'm always here...*
> *Come away my dear*
> *Let us fly*
> *Away from here*

*Until we die...*

Miss Hawley shook her head. "No, that's a new one for me, but you have such a pretty voice."

"I've been singing that as long as I can remember," Cora replied in a far away voice as she watched the spindle turn inside the music box.

As the melody tinkled out, Miss Hawley rubbed her fingers across the polished inlaid wood design. "This is a fine gift, Cora," she said. "So, please tell me what happened?"

Snapping back to the here and now, Cora took a deep breath. She couldn't *tell*. She stood up and stepped away from her desk. Turning her back to Miss Hawley, she grasped the folds of her skirt and lifted them. But she could *show*.

"Oh dear Lord!" the woman gasped, seeing the now blackening bruises that striped the backs of Cora's legs. "Oh my God!"

Cora dropped her skirt and turned around. "God? She did it in His name!" And began to wail once more as the woman folded her into her arms.

That night, Barbara Hawley got well and truly drunk as she sat in the sitting room of her one bedroom apartment. It didn't take much to accomplish that feat—the last time she had anything to drink was almost a year ago when she celebrated the ringing in of the New Year. From this very same chair.

She had taken Cora to the School Nurse, who applied a salve and covered the nasty welts. The poor thing spent the rest of the school day there while Barbara had a terrible row with Principal Larry Burns. The nurse had summoned him and even though the bruises on Cora's legs were plain as day, he forbade Barbara from notifying Children's Aid.

"The child was disciplined by her parents, and while she has light bruising, she's in no danger, Miss Hawley," he said. They were in his office, he behind his desk, speaking with authority.

Barbara leapt to her feet. "Light bruising! That girl was beaten!" She pointed a finger at the man. "Beaten like a dog!"

Mr. Burns shook his head slowly. "No. There is no bleeding, and while she may be uncomfortable for a few days, she did not sustain real, lasting physical injury." He sat back in his chair; the School Board's guidelines open on his desk. Tapping the pertinent section, he said, "There is no justification for the school to interfere with parental rights at this time. The child is in no danger."

"What? She has to come to school bleeding?" Barbara could barely contain herself. "Or with a broken arm? Is that what you're saying?" She took a deep breath. "What kind of a man are you? A child's been *beaten*!"

"Miss Hawley!" Burns leapt to his feet. "I am the Principal of this school, and you have been a teacher for only a year! Do you not think that we've encountered such episodes before? Parents have the right to care for their children as they see fit, and we have no right to interfere in such matters!"

Barbara sank to her seat before his desk. "Mister Burns, I've seen such things during my own childhood. I'm not a simpleton." She leaned forward. "This child's in real danger!"

"Based on what? On a spanking from her mother?" He shook his head.

"I know this! I can feel it in my bones! She's in danger! She needs to be removed and her parents put on notice!"

"You can *feel* it, eh?" He sat back down with a small smile.

"Yes!"

Mister Burns again shook his head slowly. With a smile more condescending than supportive, he said, "I'm sorry, Miss Hawley, but we do not operate a school, nor abrogate parental rights on such flimsy evidence as women's intuition."

"It's not that!" She leaned forward and grasped the edge of Burns' desk. "I... I *sense* things, Mr. Burns! I've never mentioned this before, but at times I..."

"Get premonitions?" he asked quietly.

"Yes!"

"Some sort of indication from inexplicable sources of ominous portents?"

"Exactly!" Thank God! There was hope the man would understand! Goodness, she didn't understand how she *knew things*, but Mr. Burns' face took on an expression of comprehension as he nodded and looked down at his desk.

Keeping his eyes down on the desk, he spoke in an even voice. "I see." He lifted his head and looked sternly at the teacher. "Miss Hawley, I hope you've simply seen too many movies. Or perhaps have read too many novels."

Barbara's face recoiled in surprise and confusion. "I...I don't understand."

"That's exactly my point, Miss Hawley." Getting to his feet, he said, "You're speaking now like someone deranged."

"What!" She leapt to her feet.

"Do not EVER come to me with such nonsense ever again! You went from women's intuition to now speaking of the supernatural!" Shaking his head he guffawed, "Ghosts and goblins, my, my." His face again went dark and he pointed to the door of his office. "This matter is settled! Good day to you, Miss Hawley!"

Sitting in her room, downing another shot of whiskey, she decided that she would call in sick to the school on Monday. Instead of teaching, she'd drive into Kingston and go to the School Board's offices. If she got no satisfaction there, it would be on to the Kingston Police Department headquarters.

Raising her glass, she toasted the full moon as the clock struck midnight. "Don't worry, Cora, your rescue is nigh," she said with a slur in her voice. Thank goodness tomorrow was Friday.

# CHAPTER
# TWENTY-SEVEN

*C*ora... wake up..."

She had drifted off while sitting on the bed.

*"The moon is full my dear. Come to me..."*

"Of course," she said out loud, tossing the covers off the bed.

Of course she would come to Mister Pooka! She had come to him every full moon for as long as she could remember! When she was a little kid, he gave her ice cream and candy. When she got bigger, he took her to the Kingston Fair, then Disney Land. They'd spend hours and hours visiting magical places, and he'd have her right back home with no one the wiser. Mister Pooka was magical like that.

And whenever Mother or Father gave her a thrashing (and they'd become more frequent the last few months) he *always* made the pain go away. She put her feet on the floor and put her sneakers back on. When she bent over to tie the laces, the backs of her legs screamed as the skin on her thighs stretched. Boy oh boy, she sure couldn't wait for him to get rid of these stings, Mother was getting as good as Father in making things hurt.

She threw on her green Sunday dress and grabbed a sweater. Mr. Pooka would make her as warm as toast when she got to the barn, but the evening had the sharp bite of winter in it despite it being June.

With years of practice, she snuck out of her room and out of the house. She carried the music box Greg had given her the day before. It was amazing; the tune it played was the same as the song she and Mister Pooka sang together every time she came to the barn to visit him. Since she was really little—three? four? — she had come to the barn on the night of the full moon.

Barn? It looked kinda like a church, with its low walls and sharply peaked roof. She thought it was prettier in the moonlight than the church she had to attend with her parents. Even though Fellowship Gospel Church was newer and cleaner, she never felt she belonged. She snorted. Mister Pooka has been welcoming her to the barn for years!

As she approached, the doors swung open silently, just wide enough for her to slip through. After she stepped inside, they arced closed again, the only sound being the click of the latch being reset.

The barn had been pitch black as she entered, but when the doors shut, as usual her 'Special Spot' on the floor began to glow. A foot wide square of light, the color a yellowy-green marked her spot on the floor in the center of the barn. She became warm as toast as soon as she stepped on it, and the pain in her legs vanished.

"Ahhh…" she said out loud. "Thank you."

She sat down on the barn floor in the center of the light as Mister Pooka drifted inside her head. She closed her eyes. An expression of pleased surprise flowered on her face. "Oh!"

As she began to drift away, she began to sing the song Mister Pooka had taught her years and years ago.

*Come away with me*
*We'll always be*
*Just me and you*
*Just us two…*
*When things go bad*
*And make you sad*
*Fear not my dear*
*I'm always here…*
*Come away my dear*
*Let us fly*
*Away from here*
*Until we die…*

*They were in an airplane! Sitting at the window seat she looked down on the city lights twinkling below, mesmerized.*

*"I've never been on an airplane!" she said.*

*"I know," Mr. Pooka replied. She turned to look at him. He was quite handsome this time. He reminded her of that man that looked after Little*

*Orphan Annie in the comic pages of the newspaper. His head was completely bald, and he had a grand smile as he looked at her.*

*"Do you like it?" he asked, his voice a deep baritone.*

*"Oh yes!" She turned back to watch the scenery unfold below. "Where are we going?"*

*Mr. Pooka chuckled. "Wherever you want, my dear!"*

*He always said that. When she would come to visit him, she could go wherever she wanted, eat whatever she desired, and do whatever she felt like. It had always been that way. Why oh why couldn't it be forever and not just on the night of the full moon? She had asked him that before, so many times, but he had always told her that the time wasn't just right.*

*She turned back to him. He was sipping a glass of champagne and watched her over the rim of the glass.*

*"May I try that?" she said.*

*Again, he chuckled. "Whatever you want, my dear," he said once more and handed her a glass. The bubbles tickled her nose, and it tasted very sweet. Like a gentle version of ginger ale, she thought.*

*When she thought again how she would like this to be forever, her mouth turned down.*

*"What's the matter, my dear?" Mr. Pooka asked, his dark eyes narrowing in concern.*

*She decided to act more grown up. "Oh, the same as usual. I'd like us to be here in this forever, but you keep telling me it's not the time yet."*

*"I see," he said. "And how are things going?"*

*"TERRIBLE!" she burst out. "Mother beat me terribly yesterday! I could hardly walk!"*

*"You're joking!" he said.*

*"No! I'm not! My legs hurt, and Mother said I got just what I deserved! She hates me!"*

*Mr. Pooka grew quiet and put his glass on the tray in front of them. He turned in his seat to face her better. "But you always are such a good girl, Cora. Why is she so mean to you?"*

*"Because she hates me! She loves my brother Sean more! Father hates me even more! He's told me that he wished he had two sons, not a little harlot!"*

*"Your father called you that name?" Mr. Pooka's eyes flew open wide in disbelief.*

*"Yes! He's said it before, and I know what that word means! I looked it up in the dictionary at school! It's a bad word!" She sat thrust herself back in her*

*seat, and for the first time EVER with Mr. Pooka, she began to cry. "They hate me, Mister Pooka. I wish I was dead!" She looked over to him, to expect to see him horrified, but all he did was smile gently.*

*"Do you really believe that, Cora? They want you to die?"*

*She nodded, tears running down her cheeks.*

*"You're such a fine young lady. A sweet girl, who only wants to be loved. THEY wish you dead."*

*"Yes!" She didn't have any idea where that thought came from, but the more Mr. Pooka said it, the more true it sounded.*

*He rubbed her shoulder. She felt like an electric current passed through her. It was the first time he ever, ever touched her! Not even when she was really little, the first times she started coming to the barn to go on 'trips' with him, had he ever so much as patted the top of her head.*

*It felt wonderful. If she was a kitten, she would be purring right now. And at the same time, the hurt and sadness in her heart transformed into anger, and then a rage.*

*A killing rage.*

*She turned from Mr. Pooka to stare at the back of the seat in front of her. She felt her face get very stern, and through the thinnest lips, said, "I shouldn't die." She turned to look at Mr. Pooka, and again he had the kindest expression on his face.*

*He reached out to rub her shoulder again. "No, you shouldn't, my dear. Go o n..."*

*She gave an emphatic nod and said, "THEY should die."*

*A beam of gladness took over Mr. Pooka's face and he began clapping his hands together softly. "You're absolutely right! And if they do..."*

*Cora's eyes sprung open in happy excitement. "We can go away! Forever! Right?"*

*"Yes! We'll go tonight!" His face glowed, he was so happy for them! He patted his hands together in joy.*

Cora crept back into the house and up to her bedroom. She opened the door to her closet and rummaged around in the bottom of it. Clearing out the furthest back corner, she lay her music box there. Mr. Pooka told her that she had to do that *first*, and if she did it just so, the rest of her 'errands' would be easy-peasy. As she settled the music box into the corner, it suddenly grew warm in her hands.

The warmth travelled up her arm right to her head, and exploded in a red flash.

"Oh!" was all she could say before everything else faded away.

The girl's eyes were wide and her pupils were fully dilated as she crept back down the stairs to the kitchen. She went to the kitchen drawer where her mother stored all of her knives and opened it. In the total darkness, she easily found and pulled out the carving knife with the longest blade—it was more than ten inches long. She fished back into the drawer and pulled out the knife sharpener and ran the blade through it, making sure it was as sharply honed as possible.

She held the blade before her eyes, and in a flat voice, repeated her instructions. In a low whisper, she said, "First the boy, then summon the mother and finish off the father as he sleeps." Repeating it over and over, she climbed the stairs.

She went silent at the top of the stairs. Like a mouse she crept into the room of the boy—the boy who despised her and wanted her dead—to find him just as Mr. Pooka promised. He was flat on his back, snoring softly.

In a voice that was so soft, she said, "Now, quick, quick, quick!"

In a flash she was beside the bed. She held the point of the knife just below the boy's ribs. In a single fluid motion, with all of her strength, she drove the blade upwards under the ribcage as her other hand clamped down on the boy's mouth. She wiggled the blade back and forth for a moment, but knew as she had been told that she had driven the steel right into the boy's heart.

He didn't even have time to open his eyes before death took him. She withdrew the blade and wiped the blood off on the sheets of the bed.

"Summon the mother," she said in a dead voice as she pattered to the bedroom of the woman and man.

The door opened without so much as a squeak as had been promised. She scurried up to the side of the bed where the woman lay. She gently shook the woman, rousing her.

"Hmph... wha—"

"Mother! Come quickly! Something's the matter with Sean!" she hissed as quietly as possible. "He's not moving!"

The woman's eyes sprang open wide. She was fully awake now, the terror of something the matter with her oh so precious son driving her from the bed and to his room like a dervish. Cora was right on her heels.

The switch for the light didn't work because Cora had taken the bulb from the lamp. In the darkness the woman flew to the bedside of her precious little boy. She dropped to her knees and began to shake him.

"Quickly, quickly, quickly!" Cora whispered as she slid up behind the woman. She held the knife so the blade was horizontal, easier to slide between the ribs on the woman's back. As the woman shook and called out to the boy, Cora's fingers counted up the necessary number of ribs and slid the knife in between once again. With a savage yank of revenge, she twisted and gored the inside of the woman's chest with the steel.

The woman collapsed over the body of her precious son, as dead as he.

"Finish off the father as he sleeps," Cora said in a flat voice as she padded back to the bedroom of the woman and the man. "Quickly, quickly!"

The man was in bed in the same position as the boy had been. And was dead just as quickly. Cora left the knife jutting from his chest to return to the barn. She wiped the blood from her hands on her green dress. It didn't matter, Mr. Pooka said he'd look after everything.

In her clear sweet voice, she began to sing:

*Come away with me*
*We'll always be*
*Just me and you*
*Just us two...*
*When things go bad*
*And make you sad*
*Fear not my dear*
*I'm always here...*
*Come away my dear*
*Let us fly*
*Away from here*
*Until we die...*

Again, the barn doors swung open to greet her, and remained open after she entered. The special spot in the center of the barn floor was glowing like a green hued sun now, filling the barn with the sickly color. She stepped over onto it.

But she didn't feel the pleasant warmth and goodness. She was cold and afraid!

"Mister Pooka!" she called out. "It's done! We can fly away now!" Her voice hitched for a second. Just what had been done? She looked around the barn. The cows were as still as statues, in their stalls. A quick jab of fear pierced her heart like the blade of a knife. "Mister Pooka! Where are you?"

A raspy gravelly voice came down from the hayloft. *"I'm up here, my dear. Come to meeee..."*

She started at the sound. "What's wrong? Are you sick? What's happened?" Her hands felt sticky and she wiped them on her dress. It didn't matter. Mr. Pooka would buy her another one, a finer one when they flew away.

*"Come to meee..."* Mr. Pooka's voice was almost scary sounding. There was kindness in it, yes. But there was something else... She went to the ladder that rose up to the loft. Putting a hand and foot on the ladder, she again hesitated.

*"Coraaa... sing our song... every... thing is going.... To be wonderful. Come to me, my dear."*

His voice sounded better. Well, a little. She began to sing the lyrics, and he was right. Singing their special song always made her feel better. She sang it over and over as she climbed all the way to the topmost rung, the one right at the rafters.

Stepping off the ladder onto a rafter, she looked down. She was so high up! Father had forbidden her to ever climb up to the top of the hayloft ladder. She stared down at the green glow from her special spot that looked so far away. Oh no! It was dimming! The barn was growing dark.

"Mister Pooka! I'm afraid!" She clutched the rail of the ladder with all her might. She began to feel a little dizzy as the light in her special spot on the ground began to now pulse.

Mr. Pooka's voice filled the barn. *"Are you ready, my dear? To fly away with me?"*

She looked around wild eyed. She was scared now. Really, really scared! "Where are you?" Something terrible had happened inside the house, but she didn't know what.

*"All is well, my dear."* Mister Pooka now appeared. Cora's jaw dropped. He was floating in mid air! He smiled warmly again at the expression on her face. *"Surprise! We really can fly, Cora!"*

"You... you're flying! Just like Superman on the TV!" she gasped.

He chuckled. *"And you can too!"* He held out his arms. *"Let's fly away together, Cora! Forever!"*

"Really?"

*"Oh yes! It's so easy!"* He did a spin in the air. "And so much fun!" He held out his arms. "Let's fly away now!"

With a "Wheeee!" Cora leapt from the ladder to his waiting arms.

*"Oops!"* Mister Pooka laughed as the girl's exultation became a shriek, silenced by the crunch of her body hitting the ground.

# CHAPTER
# TWENTY-EIGHT

*Present day...*

Paige cast a glance at Amanda before taking Julian's hand and following Barbara out of the kitchen. Every muscle in her body was tight, wound like a coil as she watched the old woman. What if this didn't work? What if the only thing they accomplished was making Cora even angrier? As for whatever spirit was in the barn... She sighed. That place was probably going to be the hardest. She knew this from the hard ache deep in her gut.

They stopped in the hallway. "Wave the smudge in the air, Paige." Barbara wet her finger with the holy water and walked over to the wall. She made the sign of the cross, rubbing her damp finger along the surface of the wall. "In Jesus' name, I ask that this home be blessed. Any entity or spirit...you have no place here. I order you to leave, in Jesus' name."

Her voice was firm yet gentle, a loving way that you would speak to a child that you needed to correct. Paige could feel her body ease and she held her head high waving the wand of smoldering sage. Was she imagining it or was the air becoming lighter despite the wafts of acrid smoke drifting higher to the ceiling?

After moving in a counter circle around the room, repeating the gesture and prayer, Barbara turned to Julian. "Pour the line over the kitchen entrance first and then the other one, going into the front foyer."

Julian looked up at Paige and she nodded. He scooped the canister from the crook of his arm and body and holding it like a chalice, he walked over and poured the first line. Barbara led the way from the room and stood in the front foyer, looking up the stairway to the floor above. When Julian stepped into the space near Paige his hands trembled pouring the line of salt in the second doorway.

Musical notes sounded, the tinny familiar tune of the music box. Paige gasped. It was barely audible coming from the front bedroom upstairs, but when Barbara's gaze darted to meet hers, it was obvious she'd heard it too. Julian once more held the canister close to his body and scrambled to Paige's side to take her hand. The music stopped as abruptly as it had started.

"It's Cora. She's trying to scare us again." Julian whispered and snuggled in close to Paige's thigh.

Barbara looked down at him and there was sadness in her face. "Yes. She's a scared, lost girl, Julian. She's frightened of leaving, frightened by the religious teachings of her parents, of hell...after what she did."

A thundering boom resounded from the upstairs. Paige jumped and Julian clutched her thigh, dropping the container of salt and hiding his face against her leg.

"Paige? Julian?" Amanda's voice pierced the air. Underlying that was the sound of Avril crying.

Paige's mouth had gone completely dry while her heart was a race horse. "We're okay!" Under her breath, she muttered, "so far." Holding the sage smudge high and away from Julian, she bent and hugged him close. "It's okay, buddy. We'll be okay. I won't let anything happen to you, but we need to do this."

When Barbara walked over to the wall continuing the ritual with the holy water, Paige rose and followed, waving the smudge smoke.

"Julian, you may pour salt along the outside doorway." The old lady nodded her head, watching him intently. "We all know that it's the upstairs that Cora haunts but we need to cleanse these rooms so that she won't want to come down here."

Paige stepped closer to Julian, watching him as he completed his task. He needed to know she was right there next to him and that's the way it would stay. She turned to Barbara, "The living room is another room Cora's been in. She keeps flipping a picture around making sure we know she's there."

"Poor Cora." Barbara clucked her tongue and continued on into the living room. She paused at the picture hanging by the corner of its frame and adjusted it.

Paige rolled her eyes. It was hard to feel sorry for Cora, especially since she was the cause of so much terror since they'd moved in. She took Julian's hand again and followed Barbara into the living room. When she passed the picture on the wall, an icy chill swept through her neck and shoulders. Julian squeezed her hand and his eyes were like saucers when she looked down at him. He'd felt it too.

"We'll start at the far wall. Any spiritual imprints and entities besides Cora's will be able to escape to the upstairs as we cleanse each room." She paused mid-step and turned to look at Paige. "Have you been in the attic? Is the entrance accessible?"

Paige's eyebrows drew together and she sighed. "I think there's a hatch." She nodded. "Yeah. At the far end of the hallway, there's a hatch with a handle. Maybe there're stairs that pull down." She peered at the old woman. "Why?"

"We need to do every room. Even ones that aren't used." She walked over to the wall and doused her finger with holy water, making the sign of the cross and repeating her prayer.

Paige adjusted the smudge bundle laying in the bowl, so that the embers were free of the glass. Holding the two, she waved it in the air behind Barbara. She pointed to a door on the far side of the room. "Don't forget that room. It's where the furnace and electrical panel and all that stuff is. The house is built on a slab of concrete."

"Thanks." Barbara turned and walked over to the other room's entrance.

When she disappeared inside, Paige grabbed Julian's hand and the two of them followed. She ducked a cobweb that fluttered in the air, caught in the glow of the hanging light bulb. Barbara was already on the other side next to the furnace. Aside from the creepy spiders and centipedes that probably claimed this room as their own, the room seemed free of any supernatural vibrations.

They finished the utility room and living room and were about to go up the stairs when an icy blast of air swooped down the stairwell. It wasn't just the chill that made goose bumps skitter across Paige's skin. This was a malevolent warning to them.

How bad was it going to be up there?

# CHAPTER TWENTY-NINE

O h God, this was it. They'd completed the cleansing of the other rooms upstairs and now, there was just her room left to do. Cora's lair. Paige's stomach roiled and she barely dared to breathe following Barbara down the hallway.

Just as Barbara was about to enter, the door slammed shut with its strongest 'THUD' ever. She bounced backward to avoid it. The old woman seemed to falter for a moment, bending slightly and bracing herself with her hand against the jamb.

Paige forced herself to step closer. The air was thick and even colder there and the hair on the back of her neck was standing straight up. "Barbara...?" She clutched Julian's hand, shielding him behind her legs.

The old lady looked down at the floor for a moment. Her face was ashen and tight. "I just need to take a moment and rest. This is not going to be easy." She forced a weak smile, which was meant to be reassuring, but failed miserably.

"I'm scared, Aunt Paige." Julian tugged on Paige's shirt before taking a step backwards.

The music box started to play once more, its notes playing rapidly, like bullets from a machine gun.

BANG! BANG!

The closed room door vibrated from objects being hurled against it from the other side. The sounds struck horror in Paige's gut. Cora knew what was coming and was throwing a tantrum.

Barbara took a deep breath and her chin rose. She grasped the doorknob and turned it. Putting her shoulder to it, she pushed it open wide.

Paige's jaw dropped at the mayhem inside. The drawers in the dresser were opening and shutting with a force that shook the sturdy wood. Clothes and bedcovers floated in the air and then fell in a heap. All the while, the tinny melody of the music box played on, perfectly centered on the dresser.

How could this be? It was a madhouse. She stepped backwards, bumping into Julian.

With love and authority blending in her voice, Barbara called out, "In Jesus' name, I command you to stop this." She strode forward holding the bottle of holy water before her like a sword.

In a flash the music box flew from the dresser; Barbara ducked her head, and it slammed into her shoulder. The old lady stumbled to the side, gripping the top of the dresser to keep from falling. Her hand holding the bottle of holy water began to tremble.

She let out a cry of pain as her arm was yanked above her head. Paige watched in dumbstruck horror as the woman's fingers, one by one were peeled back from the vessel.

"NO!" Paige screamed. She ran to Barbara and folded her own hands over the woman's fingers. As soon as she did, a spear of the coldest sensation she had ever experienced shot through her chest. She howled in surprise, pain and terror, but held Barbara's hand with all her might. Through gritted teeth, she managed to snarl, "Be gone Cora! The will of God commands you!"

Her words energized Barbara, who lifted her head. "Dear Cora, poor, poor Cora..." Her voice choked, "I'm sorry for all you've been through... I forgive you for what you did... God forgives you, Cora... you must move on..." her voice faded in a rasp.

The bedlam in the room faltered slightly for a moment, then resumed with a burst of energy. Shoes, books, hairbrushes and framed photos peppered the two women as they stood with their heads ducking out of the way.

"LEAVE US ALONE!" with a scream, Julian flew into the room and grasped the women's hands in his own. "You're being mean!" he cried into the air. "Stop it! Stop being so damn mean!" He began to shake the bottle back and forth over his head, and more of the blessed water squirted from its nozzle around the room.

In reply, a guttural roar enveloped the room, its grinding, gnashing sound scraping the very air. It went on and on as the three of them, hands joined gaped about. The roar wavered into a wail, a pealing keen of agony, sadness... and regret. As the sound pierced their ears the maelstrom in the room began to ebb; the spinning vortex of clothing spiraled down, coming to a rest on the floor.

The keening sound faded into a wail... and then the harsh sobs and tears of a broken hearted twelve-year-old girl, until that too faded away...

Into silence.

The music box bounced and came to rest next to her foot, the tune suddenly silent.

Barbara slumped to her knees.

Paige dropped beside her. "Are you hurt?"

"Oh my..." Barbara's hand was upon her chest. "Oh my, oh my..." she repeated, her head down as she gulped for air.

Julian had dropped to the floor as well, not letting go of the woman's hand. "You'll recover, Barbara," he said in a voice well beyond his years. "You've been brave, and good, and I have always loved you so."

Barbara blinked at Julian. "Andrew?" she gasped in a whisper.

Julian smiled. "Aye, but only for a trice. I'll be taking the wee one along to where she belongs now." He bent and kissed the side of the old woman's cheek. "I told you I'd love you forever, now didn't I, lass?" Taking his lips from her face, he said, "Now kiss me once and let me go."

"I've done this before, no?"

"Aye," he said sadly.

With tears flowing, Barbara leaned in and kissed Julian's cheek. Tilting her head back, she said, "Fare thee well, love."

"Aye. Fare thee well..." Julian's voice faded, and his face took on a serene expression as he closed his eyes. Opening them, he said, "*Father* Andrew?"

Nodding, Barbara dabbed at her eyes with her sleeve. "My first, and *only* true love from bygone days. With a nod to Julian and Paige, they helped her to her feet.

When she was steadier, Barbara said, "We're far from done. Let's complete the blessing of this home." She stepped over to the first wall and blessed it with the holy water. With a nod to Paige, she continued to the other wall.

Paige's heart was pounding so fast and hard, she didn't know if she would faint or explode. She waved the wand of sage, following the old lady. The silence in the room was palpable...with a sense of the surreal after what had just happened. Could it really have worked so quickly?

When Barbara stepped into the closet Paige held her breath. Oh Lord, let this work! She seemed to be taking a long time. Julian stepped over to stand beside his aunt, looking at the dark opening of the closet with wide eyes.

Barbara stepped out and smiled at them. "Julian, you may pour the salt over the closet doorway now."

Paige blew a long sigh and continued with the smudging. It looked like this was doing the trick!

Barbara moved slowly to finish the other walls and then stepped out into the hall, directing Julian to salt the door to Paige's room.

"There. Can you sense it too?" Barbara smiled at Paige.

Paige's mouth fell open and she grinned. It was true. No longer did she feel like she was being watched...the air was warmer...no thickness in the atmosphere anymore! "Yeah! That's it? She's gone?"

Julian finished pouring the salt and he joined the two of them in the hallway. "I don't feel her anymore, Aunt Paige."

"We're not done yet, you two. There's still the attic and..." Barbara looked down at Julian. "Don't worry, son. You've been a brave boy." She turned to Paige. "Now where is this entrance to the attic? Somehow, I think doing it is going to be more of a formality, but let's finish."

Paige rose on the tips of her toes and grasped the handle of the attic entrance. At first it refused to budge. She yanked harder and sank to her knees, using her body weight. With a jerk it let go and she had to scramble out of the way of the stairs that folded to the floor. A piece of cellulose insulation fluttered from the yawning dark hole above.

She watched Barbara slowly climb the stairs. It was true what Barbara had said about it being a formality. Aside from the darkness, the air falling softly from the upper space felt normal. And the sense that it was clear of anything malevolent, drifted through her body like a warm breeze relaxing her muscles. She stepped up the stairs and onto the rough hewn platform. She could barely make out the old woman, relying more on the sound of her voice as she blessed the walls.

She almost stumbled when her foot hit some wooden boxes and she reached out to steady herself. Going slower now, she continued, waving the sage smudge before her.

Barbara turned and started walking back to the opening. "That's it, my dear. We need to seal the opening with salt and we're done. She led the way down the pine steps. At the bottom, she took the salt from Julian. She handed the canister up to Paige and smiled. "There's hardly room on the stairs. You do this."

Paige balanced the smudge and managed to line the edges of the opening before turning and going back down to join the others. Her jaw tightened when she looked down the hallway towards her room. There was still one thing that made her uneasy. Where it had all started.

She turned to Barbara. "Will you take the music box? Even if all of this worked, I don't want it here anymore. It was Cora's and you knew her. I think she would want you to have it."

"It's a beautiful piece of work. Yes. I'll take it." The old woman's eyes welled with tears and she walked down the hall. When she returned she held the music box. "Thank you."

# Chapter Thirty

A short while later, everyone was assembled in the kitchen. There was calmness in the air. It was as if they needed a break, ignoring the fact that the hardest part lay ahead—the barn.

Paige felt like a dishrag that had been used and hung out to dry. And, looking across the counter at Barbara, the strain was also telling on the old lady. One shoulder drooped lower than the other—probably still hurting from the blow from the music box.

"Are you sure that's all you'd like? A boiled egg and toast?" Amanda set the food down in front of Barbara, next to her mug of tea.

Matt was busy stirring the old standby, a pot of boiling noodles for macaroni and cheese. "She eats like a bird. I try to have dinner with her once a week to see that she doesn't starve."

"I'm fine. I just need a little something before we start in the barn." She took a nibble of toast, smiling over at her nephew.

Amanda grinned and shook her head. "I can hardly believe you've fixed it! Wow! The house is free...no more banging and footsteps? No more spooky stuff happening?" She scooped her arm around the old lady's shoulders and hugged her gently. "If only you could fix Josh's problem at work."

Paige got the bowls down from the cabinet for the 'mac'n cheese' and set them next to Matt. She turned to her sister and smiled. "See? Things are looking up. Don't worry; Josh's problem will be fixed too." Her voice was cheery despite the fact that her stomach was in knots. There was still the barn to do. She'd be just fine and dandy if they left the barn for the next day.

Barbara swallowed and then she nodded at Amanda. "Things will work out. Trust in yourself and your husband and of course, God. We all need a little of His help." She looked down at the table and her smile was sad. "I'm glad that I was able to help poor Cora. Maybe now she'll find the love she so desperately sought when she was alive."

Paige noticed the red scrapbook sitting on the desk where she'd put it when they got home. "In the library earlier, you said that there was more to this than a haunting. What did you mean? The scrapbook with all the newspaper clippings...that's part of what you were saying, right?"

Barbara looked over at the two kids, and Matt who was placing bowls of yellow noodles before them. She looked at Paige and shook her head. "We'll talk about that later. Suffice it to say, that there are times and places when the veil between this realm and the afterlife become thinner than usual. Not everything in that realm is of God. There are forces that work to undermine goodness."

She snorted. "Not that mankind needs a lot of help in being bad, or greedy, or cruel, it would seem. Still...some horrible things happen during certain precarious times. I fear we are close to one of those times, if not actually in it right now."

The red scrapbook had clippings that Paige had only skimmed but she recalled a couple. "Are you saying that the tragedies, Martin Luther King's death and Robert Kennedy's...that it was during a time when the veil was thin? That..." She pantomimed quotation marks with her fingers, "...'evil' was a strong force in the world?"

Matt set a bowl of noodles in front of Paige. "Both of those guys died in 1968." He looked over at his aunt. "When did Cora and her family die? Was it '68 as well?"

She nodded and continued eating, looking down at the table for a few moments.

"But that could be just coincidence. Tragedies happen all the time. For you to say that Cora was influenced and what happened here was because of the year...well, it's just so far-fetched. Coincidence, that's all." Amanda stood behind Avril, finger combing the child's hair from the sides of her face.

Barbara nodded. "Yes. You've got a point. But the other one. Elmer Larkspur. The year was 1939—Hitler, Mussolini, the Holocaust. There was a world war and a heinous despot killing many innocent people."

Paige's jaw tightened and she swallowed hard. She wanted to believe Amanda that it was just coincidence. But the niggling knot of certainty deep in her gut was saying Barbara was right. The fact that the old woman felt we were close to another time of weakening in that veil made her skin crawl...especially with the barn left to do.

Twenty minutes later, Barbara ruffled Julian's hair, and she looked down at him. "You did well, son. I know you don't want to go out to the barn." She smiled. "You don't have to. Matt can take your place now. You stay here with your mother and sister."

He looked up at her and his eyes welled with tears. He shook his head. "I don't want to go out there, but I think I need to. That one in the barn is really bad." He sighed and looked down at his shoes for a moment. "But I wouldn't mind if Matt came too."

Paige's hand froze mid air as she was about to set a new bundle of sage alight. Her blood ran cold, coursing through her veins. Julian's words echoed her own fear. She looked over at Barbara and Matt. The nervous discomfort was in their eyes as well.

# Chapter Thirty-One

The tapestry bag containing the salt canister thudded against Matt's thigh as he walked to the barn. One hand held a powerful flashlight and the other grasped his aunt's elbow steadying and guiding her along the flagstone path.

Behind them, Paige held the smoldering smudge before her, stepping carefully and with fearful reluctance, in the low light. Julian's hand was small and warm in hers, walking close beside her.

"It doesn't hurt to say a prayer you know. That goes for all of you." Barbara glanced over her shoulder at Paige. "You do believe in God, don't you?"

Paige's eyes went wider still. The fact that the old lady was actually talking about God now that they were about to enter the barn was added confirmation of the danger there. "Yes. Of course I believe...it's just that I kind of stopped going to church. Amanda and I were raised Roman Catholic."

"Join the club." Matt snorted and then turned to smile at her.

Paige squeezed Julian's hand and then looked back at Matt. "But you believe in a higher power, don't you Matt? I mean...I do. There's got to be something greater than us which created this. And it stands to reason, that if what we're experiencing now, this ghost stuff...well, it's proof to me that there is life after death."

Although Paige shivered in the cool night air, it wasn't just the September weather making her shiver. If she were to be honest with herself, she had to admit that. And if honesty was armor, then she'd better own it tonight.

"Good. You don't have to attend church to ask for divine help." Barbara stopped a few feet away from the barn doors that were once more hanging slightly ajar. "It's strong in there. Julian, you are right. I can feel the hatred inside, already."

The little boy nodded and sidled closer to Paige.

Paige took a step forward, so that the four of them were now facing the barn doors. A faint smell of rotten meat drifted into her nostrils making her stomach roll, threatening to erupt the 'mac 'n cheese' right there and then.

"Lord of Light, protect us." Barbara whispered and took a deep breath.

"Amen to that." Matt stepped forward focusing the beam of light into the gap between the doors. He turned to Paige. His face was tight and a line dissected between his heavy dark eyebrows. "There're lights and electricity in there, right?"

"Yes. It's on the right hand side, next to the door frame." Her gaze flickered to where the beam of light sliced the darkness. An icy bead of sweat slithered down her spine, as she thought of going in there, confronting whatever. Barbara was right. Lord protect them. Her grip on Julian's hand grew tighter still.

"Goin' in." He stepped forward and immediately the beam of the flashlight flitted to the right, leaving only the glowing orange tips of her sage smudge breaking the night.

After a moment, golden light filled the space and Barbra turned to Julian and Paige. "Ready?"

"No. But we have to do this." It came out like a croak from her suddenly dry mouth.

Matt appeared in the opening, pushing the door on the left wide for his aunt to enter. He reached his hand and guided her inside. When Paige stepped through, his eyes met hers for a moment. The tight dread mirrored her own.

The smell was worse in there and the air seemed thick, like sickly green pea soup on her skin. She covered her nose and mouth with her hand.

"Yuck." Julian's other hand rose to pinch his nostrils shut.

Paige looked down at him and grimaced, holding his hand while they followed Barbara, her other hand wafting the acrid smudge smoke. The hanging light bulb did a poor job of lighting the entire open space of the ancient barn, leaving the rafters and corners in heavy shadow.

Barbara wet her hand with the holy water and walked slowly to the first wall to the right. "Benedicamus Patrem sanctum locum istum." She made the sign of the cross with her finger over the coarse-grained wood.

Oh my God! Paige's heart was in her mouth hearing the words. From all the 'ums' it had to be Latin the older woman was speaking! It was that bad that Barbara felt the need to use the language of the church? She closed her eyes for a moment. Of course it was that bad. She knew it from the stench and the tight feeling in her body.

When Barbara passed by, her hand gripped Paige's arm and she murmured. "I'm blessing this space in God's name. Latin seemed more appropriate in here."

All the while, Matt stayed at Barbara's side like a guide dog, watching her every step. He cleared the way with his foot, kicking hay from the concrete floor. From the set of his jaw, the muscle working overtime, it was clear, he was as uneasy as Paige.

CLANG!

Paige jumped and clutched Julian to her stomach! On the floor behind them, only a few feet away dust motes rose above the iron hook. She looked up to see the frayed ends of the rope that had secured it to a rafter high above. Her fingers clutched her throat, barely daring to breathe air. Holy shit! That had been close!

"Lord protect us!" Barbara's eyes were round as dinner plates looking over at Paige and then Matt. "We'll need to keep an eye above us as well." She started to the other wall, shaded in darkness under the hayloft.

There was no way she could let Julian stay inside the barn! She looked down into his wide eyes, and noticed his lower lip trembling. "Julian, you need to leave. Go back to the house and stay inside with your mother."

His eyes welled with tears and he shook his head. "No. I'll be okay if I stay close to you."

Paige looked over at the open doorway, noticing the wide beamed frame. There was something she'd read about being in door openings if there was an earthquake.... "Stand next to the door and run if anything else falls or happens in here. I'll keep an eye on you. But I'd really rather that you went back to the house."

He shook his head again but walked over to stand in the frame of the door, watching her silently.

Every cell of Paige's body was screaming to get out of there, to scoop Julian up and run to the house with him but she managed to nod at him and keep walking. With Barbara in the lead, and Matt following, Paige made it a column of three.

Matt flipped the flashlight on, casting its beam on a series of old oil and gas cans, and worn yellow ropes hanging from spikes half way up the wall.

Paige held the burning embers closer to her body, watching and taking care that any spark landed in the bowl, not stray hay on the floor.

When Barbara started the Latin prayer, her finger moving along the wood, darkness abruptly descended. Paige gasped and froze still as a statue. The only light now was from Matt's flashlight.

"Julian? Are you okay, Babe?"

"Ye...Yes." The fear dripped from his voice in the doorway.

"I want you to go back to the house."

"Ummm..."

"Now, Jules." She thought fast. This was no place for a kid right now. Who was she kidding? She wouldn't mind bailing either. "Let your mother and sister know we're almost done here, okay?"

"Well... okay. But if you're not back soon, we'll come and get you?"

"Fair enough."

"Okay, Aunt Paige." He turned and she watched him scoot back up the path.

Paige watched and listened for the sound of the back door of the house opening and closing, then turned back towards the interior of the barn.

Barbara had continued her prayer in the dim glow from Matt's flashlight. When she was finished, she said, "Get the light again, Matt."

Paige could barely make out his face, except for the white rims around his pupils.

He strode over and flipped the light switch, flooding the area once more. His mouth dropped open and his head bobbed forward. "It was turned off! How the hell—"

"That's enough. It was turned off and that's all we need to know about that." Barbara's chin was high when she led the way to the next wall. She stopped at the space next to a wooden ladder leaning against the wooden beam bordering the hayloft.

*"Exorcizamus te, omnis immunde spiritus, omni satanica potestas, omnis incursioinfernalis adversarii, omnis legio, omnis congregatio et secta diabolica, in nomini etvirtute Domini nostri Jesu Christi."* Her voice was louder and the cross she made with her finger was larger than any she'd done up to that point.

The air seemed to crackle with a new energy, a low thrum rumbled in Paige's stomach as she looked around. It was the last wall, the final dictate for whatever was in the barn to leave. "Barbara? Do you feel that?"

Before the old lady had a chance to answer the barn doors burst fully open, slamming against the outside walls with a resounding bang.

Paige jerked back, almost dropping the sage smudge. "Barbara?" But any answer was lost in the whirlwind that rose, lifting fine dust particles in the air. It was strong, blowing her hair onto her face. Holy shit! Her hand rose and brushed her mane of hair back, her fingers circling to form a pony tail that she gripped tight to her shoulder as she withstood the whirlwind.

The wind was a howl that rushed to the open doors of the barn, raising dust devils of hay behind it. Above them the thick rope swayed fast, back and forth.

As quickly as it started, the wind stopped and stillness claimed the space.

"Matt. You may salt the back door now." Barbara turned to Paige. "Keep smudging, dear. I think the barn is free now but there's nothing wrong with a little overkill."

Paige's mouth fell open and her chest felt light. The whole room was light—the air, even the hanging bulb cast a brighter glow. "That last pra yer...it was different. What did you do?" She stared wide eyed at Barbara, remembering to wave the smudge when she saw the look of remonstrance in the old lady's eyes.

"It was different. It was a prayer of exorcism used in the church." The old lady grinned. "Thank goodness for the internet. I learn all kinds of things."

"And you memorized all those prayers?"

Barbara shrugged. "I read them once, took them to heart, and did my best, I guess."

Paige's head turned as she gaped at the barn, taking in the sensation of lightness. "I guess your best is pretty good, huh?" She turned and watched Matt finish up with the salting and then walked slowly out of the barn. "I sent Julian back to the house. The poor little guy. He was scared shitless."

Barbara snorted. "He wasn't the only one!" Nodding, she added, "This was no situation for a child."

Oh my God! It was done! The two women stood at the entrance waiting for Matt.

Barbara grinned at her nephew. "Finish the line of salt and then let's go home, boy. My cats are probably missing me like crazy."

Paige dropped the bundle of sage and then stomped her foot on it to douse the embers. She put her arms around Barbara's shoulders and hugged her gently. "Thank you so much! It's really gone, isn't it? Do you think it was that guy Elmer? Elmer Larkspur who was haunting the barn?"

There was an odd look in Barbara's eyes when she pulled back and looked at Paige. "Let's pray it was him."

"Well, who else could it be?"

Barbara looked away. "Something worse than a sick man."

# Chapter Thirty-Two

*A few days later...*

"I'm going to sweep up all this salt." Amanda reached for the broom in the pantry.

"You think we're going to be okay?" Paige asked. She was sitting at the kitchen counter surfing on her laptop.

"Are you kidding? After Josh's phone call this morning, I *know* everything's going to be fine," her sister replied with a grin. She and Josh had talked on the phone for almost an hour. Just a few days before, his job had been on the line because of a screw up with a supplier. Josh had started digging, and learned that they had been ripping off his company for years. Now, instead of being fired, he was due for a huge bonus. Their supplier was going to make a huge payment to dissuade a lawsuit. He was still stuck at work for the next few days though.

Paige nodded and looked up from her laptop that was set on the counter in the kitchen. "Yeah. Whatever Barbara did, worked for sure. Besides which, Josh will never understand when he comes home and sees all this salt around."

Amanda crossed the kitchen and started sweeping. "Yeah. I was here and I still have a hard time with it." Shaking her head, she said, "I already cleaned up the barn, and this is the last of it."

"You did the barn already?" Paige felt a sudden chill. "Why couldn't you just leave it there?"

Amanda huffed. "Because I don't want to make a big deal about it when he gets home, okay? He'll think I've lost my mind, silly."

Paige turned in her stool. "We were *both* involved, Sis. As well as Julian."

"Then he'll think we all went bonkers." She gave a small wave. "Look, Julian's just a kid, so anything he'd say would be no big deal. But I really want to play it as low key as possible, alright?" She stepped over and put a hand on Paige's arm. "We can tell him that we had the house blessed or something, and it was kind of odd, but that's all. It'll be easier to convince him if he doesn't see the salt and stuff all around, okay?"

"I don't know..."

"Paige, come on. We both know that I've had a hell of a time with depression. This was the first that Josh has been away since I started going down the tubes. If he came home to hear all about ghosts and suicides and crap, he'd get really scared, can't you see that? And not about ghosts... he'd get scared about *me*."

Paige nodded slowly. "Yeah, okay. But we ought to tell him the whole story."

"We will, don't worry. But not right away. Let him get used to me getting back on my feet. Deal?" Amanda held out her hand.

Paige shook it. "Deal."

Amanda collected the salt in the dustpan and then grinned over at Paige. "So you and Matt...where's he taking you tonight?"

Paige felt her neck grow warm and a smile spread over her face. Yeah Matt. They'd talked on the phone the last couple of evenings for hours it seemed and now she was actually going out on a real date with him—not a meeting with Barbara, followed by some kind of strange exorcism. It had been a long time since she'd felt this excited about going out with a guy.

"We're going on a dinner cruise. A sunset dinner cruise." She clicked the mouse and then turned the laptop around to face her sister. The website was from a company called 'Kingston 1000 Islands Cruises'. They did all sorts of them along the St. Lawrence River. The photos showed pictures of beautiful scenery and gorgeous sunsets. "This is it. Pretty fancy, huh? Look at the view of the islands. And dancing!"

Amanda's head drew back and she grinned from ear to ear. "Oh wow! And it's a full moon tonight. That's going to be spectacular on the water."

Paige smirked over at Amanda. "Told you things would work out, didn't I?"

Amanda took a deep breath and smiled. "Yes. And this time, I don't mind you lording that over me." She emptied the dustpan into the trash and then turned to Paige again. "What would we have done if Barbara hadn't shown up? We owe that lady big-time."

———※———

Late that night, after Paige said goodnight to Matt at the door, she crept quietly into the foyer and tiptoed across to the stairs. The house was still and the only lights left on were the ones in the foyer and over the stairway.

As she passed the entrance to the living room, she sneaked a quick glance at the picture on the wall. It was exactly right, hanging straight the way it should be. She felt her neck muscles relax. The house was clear now. No more ghosts of Cora or that guy in the barn.

She climbed the stairs and peeked in at Avril. The child was sound asleep in her crib, her arm clutching the worn rabbit into her body, a sweet smile on her face.

"Sweet dreams, kiddo," Paige whispered.

# CHAPTER THIRTY-THREE

A vril was having a wonderful dream. She was in a meadow on a warm summer's day chasing butterflies. She was with a very, very nice man. He was old, like she thought her grandfather would be if she had any. And he was really nice, as nice as Santa was at the mall when she visited him last winter. He made her laugh by doing tricks, and gave her nice things to eat. Even though she wasn't hungry, they tasted so good!

She loved Mister Pooka, even if he had a funny sounding name.

*"Do you like it here, Avril?" he asked, as they sat in the warm grass looking down the meadow to a pretty stream below.*

*"Oh yes!" she said, looking up at him. It was hard to see his face, even though it was daytime, but she didn't mind. She looked down to the stream. The water looked so cool and sweet.*

*"It is very cool, and very sweet," Mr. Pooka said.*

*Avril turned back to him. "How did you know I was thinking that?" she asked with a laugh.*

*"I heard you," he said. She couldn't see his face very good, but he had a nice smile.*

*"How could you hear me if I didn't say it?"*

*"Beeee-cawwwse," he said, with a chuckle, as he leaned forward and pointed to her chest, "I listened to your heart!"*

*"Oh." She turned back to the stream, and wished she saw rabbits and deer come to it to take a drink.*

*Just then, a bunny hopped out of the bushes and a baby deer stepped carefully from the woods. They looked up at her, and then leaned their heads and began to sip the clear water rustling over the rocks by the edge of the stream.*

*"Oh!" she said and clapped her hands. She looked back to Mr. Pooka and smiled. "You did that too!" When he nodded, she hugged him. His hands felt*

*a little funny as they stroked her hair at first. Then they felt nice when she closed her eyes...*

*Avril...*

She blinked her eyes, and sat up in bed. That was a very nice dream. Mister Pooka is a very nice man.

*Avril...*

She heard his voice in her head still! That was nice.

*You're nice.*

"You're still here!" she said, looking around her room. "Where are you?"

*I'm waiting for you, my dear. You can visit with me for real, but only tonight. You must hurry though.*

"Where? Are you downstairs?"

*Shhh... you need to keep quiet as a mouse or you'll ruin the surprise!*

"A surprise?" She could hear the smile in his voice.

*Yesss... for your Mommy and Daddy! Would you like to give them a surprise?*

"Oh yes!"

*Then quick like a bunny and quiet as a mouse, come down to the barn!*

"Of course!" She scrambled to the side of her bed, put on her bunny slippers and bathrobe. It was chilly, but just a little bit.

*Don't worry about it being cold, dear—the closer you get to the barn, the toastier you'll be! She felt the slightest breath of the warm summer air from the meadow brush across her face and giggled. Let's have an adventure!*

"Okay!" she whispered. And quick like a bunny and quiet as a mouse she crept from her room, down the stairs and out the door towards the barn.

As she went up the pathway, she saw how pretty the stars were and marveled at how bright the moon was. When she came up to the barn, the two doors opened all by themselves! A greeny, kinda yellowy light glowed inside and she entered, giggling.

*We're going to play a game...*

# Chapter Thirty-Four

J ulian was dreaming too, but his was not a happy one. He was thrashing in his bed, sweating and afraid.

*He was in the barn watching a crazy man. The man's hair was wild and stringy, and he had a beard that splayed down his face. He was wearing a blue work coat that had rips and tears, and blue jeans that were filthy and ripped.*

*But it was his eyes that were terrifying. Tiny black pupils were in the center of big white eyeballs. They looked straight at Julian.*

*"I know yer here!" the man said, spittle running out of the side of his mouth. "Don't matter none. Yer too late! The Lord of Darkness will have his chapel and everything will be well!*

*He had a board in his hand and strode over to the wall beside the barn doors. Light from a full moon poured through it. The man was wearing a canvas carpenter's apron. He took a pen knife from one of the pockets. Opening it, he ran the blade across his palm.*

*"Every board has a drop of my blood on it, as ordered by The Master. This last board has the most," he said aloud as he smeared the board. He then took nails and a hammer from another pocket and banged the board in place.*

*It was Elmer Larkspur!*

*He then strode to the center of the barn and spread out his arms. "All for you, my Master! The work is done!" he bellowed.*

*At his feet, the ground glowed. A square of light, a foot across shone from the very dirt of the barn, pulsing with a sickly yellowish green light.*

*Julian stood transfixed in terror watching as a whirlwind of straw and dust enveloped the man. When it subsided, Elmer was holding a shotgun.*

*"For you! For you! Always for you My Master!" he shouted as he left the barn. Julian was frozen by the doorway as the man approached. Elmer stopped before the boy and grinned.*

*As Julian stared into the now black empty eye sockets of the man, a purple haze washed over the scene. It began to billow and pulse with red highlights, and then cleared...*

*Now Avril was in the barn in her jammies. She was smiling as she climbed up the ladder at the back of the barn towards the hayloft. Just as she was about to climb the last rung, with a laugh she turned and leapt from the ladder head first.*

"NO!" He shot up out of bed and ran from his room.

# CHAPTER THIRTY-FIVE

Paige had also been sleeping fitfully. She didn't like it when Amanda had removed the salt barriers from the doorways in the house and barn. Barbara had said that the barn should be destroyed and the only barrier of protection they had from it was gone.

She shot out of bed when Julian's cry shot through her mind. By the time she got to the door of her bedroom, he was already down the stairs. He made hardly a sound, but the cries of 'Avril! Avril!' echoed in her mind anyway.

"Oh no!" She flew after him. She'd catch up to him by the time they got to the barn.

The doors of the barn were shut tight. Together, they pulled and strained at the handle, inching it open with agonizing slowness.

They could hear Avril's voice inside. She was singing something, but they couldn't make out the words.

But they both knew the tune—the same melody from the music box.

At that moment a crack of greenish light appeared in the doorway. "Demon light!" Julian hissed through his teeth. Holding the door handle as tight as he could, he braced his feet on the other side. Straining with all his might, he heaved with his legs.

The door sprang open and they both fell to the ground. Before it could close again, they bolted inside.

"Oh thank God!" Julian wheezed. Avril was still sitting in the center of the barn, right on top of the square of light below her. He ran to her and grabbing her under her arms pulled her off the ground.

Avril gave a shriek of surprise, and the world fell in.

From the spot where she had been sitting, a blast of dirt blew straight up in the air. On the ground, the square of light shone like a searchlight. At the same time a deep throaty roar of rage consumed the room. Avril, now terrified clamped her hands over her ears. An overwhelming blast of wind knocked the three of them to the ground. Tumbling and rolling they were pitched backwards to the now shut doors of the barn.

Both Avril and Julian wet themselves as they tried to hide their heads from the howling wind.

Julian struggled to his feet and staggering against the wind shouted "We have to break the stone!" Another cyclone blast knocked him back to the ground. He continued to crawl on his hands and knees towards the light in the center of the room. "Aunt Paige! We have to break the stone!"

With what? Paige gawped about the barn madly, looking for something, anything they could use as a hammer. The light from the room fully illuminated the barn's interior, but she could hardly see from the dust and crap in the air that wind was kicking up.

Kicking up!

She spun around to the doors of the barn. The horseshoe that Josh had found in the barn and nailed to the lintel of the doorway was still there.

She leapt up at it, her fingers grasping onto it. In no time she was able to twist and pull it off the wall. She turned back to the light source. Julian was on his hands and knees batting at the ground with his fists.

She struggled up beside him. The light coming up from the floor was so bright, even closing her eyes wasn't enough. But it had to do. She smashed the horseshoe down onto the ground with all her might, feeling it bounce off a smooth hard surface.

The howl became a shriek of pain as she bashed the surface again and again.

Her final blow cracked the stone, releasing the loudest thunderclap God had ever imagined. The noise alone flipped her and Julian over onto their backs.

And the barn became pitch black.

Paige lay on her back gasping for breath. She reached out and felt for Julian.

"You okay?" she asked.

She felt him struggle to his feet. "Avril!" was all he said.

Paige got to her feet. She didn't know which way was which. She slowly turned in a circle calling out to the child.

They both heard the soft cries from the area by the doors. Bumping into each other, they stumbled and clabbered their way to her.

Finding her with her hands, Paige lifted the toddler up. With one hand she pushed at the door of the barn and it opened with a piercing creak.

The pathway to the house was bathed in moonlight. As they came out of the barn, Amanda, holding a flashlight was making her way down.

"What the hell just happened?" she asked.

"Hell's got a lot to do with it, Mom," Julian said. He took the flashlight and went back to the house leaving the others at the barn.

"What is he talking about?" Amanda asked as she took Avril. The child was fast asleep, sucking her thumb. "And what in the world are you three doing out here wandering around at this time of night?"

Paige peered at her sister. "Didn't you hear Julian screaming? And running outside?"

Amanda's face screwed up. "No! What the hell are you talking about?" The two women began to walk back to the house.

Before Paige could begin to explain, Julian returned down the path. He was carrying the barbeque lighter from the unit beside the house and the gasoline can from the garden shed where they were storing the lawnmower.

"Julian Jenkins! What are you doing?"

"We have to burn down the barn, Aunt Paige," he said, ignoring his mother.

"What! You'll do no such thing!" She reached for the gas can, but Julian skittered backwards. Amanda, still holding Avril in one arm swiped at the boy again. "Paige, stop him!"

"Hold on, little buddy," Paige said. "We got to explain it to your mom."

"But then we're going to do it, right?" Julian's eyes were fierce. "Each board that place was built with is stained with the blood of Elmer Larkspur!" He waved the hand holding the barbeque lighter at the structure. "I know what that place is now! It was *never* a barn!" He turned to Amanda. "It's a church!"

"What!" Amanda's eyes followed his. "Julian..."

"It's a church for the devil! And the devil took over Elmer Larkspur when he went broke, then took over Cora Slipp, and tried to get Avril!" He turned to Paige. "Help me explain to her, Aunt Paige!"

Paige nodded slowly. "Did you see all that in your dream, Julian?" When the boy nodded back, she turned to her sister. "That's good enough for me. Amanda, as soon as we took the salt away, whatever was in there tried to get Avril." She stepped over to Julian and put her arm around his shoulder.

"He woke up and ran out to rescue her." She sighed. "Some of us in the family have a sort of gift, you know that."

"Paige, I can't take any more!" Amanda clutched her daughter to her chest.

"I know. But you have to come with us. Then you'll understand."

"No!"

"Amanda! This ends tonight! Now!" Paige took her sister by the arm and pulled her back to the barn. "You'll see the proof."

"What is it?"

"I don't know. I think it's a portal of some sort."

"We have to smash it, Aunt Paige. Then throw all the pieces into the lake." Julian's voice was low and steady, as if he was in a trance. She saw his eyes. They were gazing off into space. "It wasn't the devil himself, Aunt Paige, it was one of his minions."

"It was Mister Pooka," Avril said from her mother's arms. "He was nice at first, but then got really scary when you guys came for me." She ducked her head down into her mother's breast again. "He's gone now. He went through the doorway in the floor."

"POOKA?" Amanda asked. "Was that his name, darling?" She softly rubbed the back of her child's head.

"Yes," the reply was muffled. "He called me in my sleep tonight. He's magic or something. We had such fun at first..." She lifted her head. "I don't want him around anymore."

"And that's his name. Pooka."

"If we close the portal, Mom, all will be as it should," said Julian.

"Let's go." Amanda began to stride towards the barn.

"Whoa!" said Paige, trotting to catch up. "What got you onside?"

"That beast's *name*! That horrible, horrible beast!" They went through the barn door, Amanda in the lead. "This is OUR HOME you bastard!" she cried out to the walls and rafters. "You stay down in your pit!"

Julian came up beside her and shone the flashlight onto the ground in the center of the barn. "That's the portal, Mom. I think Elmer made it... but I think he had some help or something."

On the floor, recessed into the packed dirt was a square of stone the size of a floor tile. It was mottled with green, and yellowish green swaths of color throughout, the color of bile and dying plants. A disgusting odor wafted up from it. Two large cracks ran through it where Paige had smashed it moments before.

It was etched. A circle had been made that touched the edge of each side of the square. Inside the circle was a five-pointed star.

"Oh my God!" Paige gasped. "It's a Pentacle!"

"An upside-down Pentacle. That makes sense," said Amanda. Her voice was rock steady and ice cold. She passed Avril to her sister and squatted down. She picked up the horseshoe and began to smash it down onto the stone. "Get thee back demon!" she shouted. "Never again here!" She kept pounding the stone until it was reduced to a collection of small rocks. When she was done, she said to Julian, handing him the flashlight "Go to the house and get one of the packing boxes we used. They're in the spare bedroom."

"Thanks, Mom!" Julian then took off running.

Amanda stood up and took Avril back in her arms. "Turn on the lights, Paige. I don't know where the switch is."

Paige was able to stumble around in the dim light from the moon coming through the door and turned on the light.

"Okay, I'll bite. What tipped you off that this is for real?"

"Pooka. That's what they call a demon in Ireland." Amanda shook her head. "I had a friend in my dorm when I was away at college who was pretty weird. Lindsay was into Satanism for a while."

"Whaaa—"

Amanda waved her free hand. "It wasn't me, but we did talk about it. It got kind of weird for her, and she backed off big-time. I remember when she was in it, she wore an amulet. It was made of the same stuff as that."

"What is that?"

Amanda snorted. "It's called 'Serpentine' believe it or not. She pointed with her chin at the debris. "And that amulet she wore had the same symbol as what was on that crap over there." She turned back to Paige. "It's the Satanic symbol."

"Yeah, I've seen it before."

Amanda shook her head slowly. "But the thing that got me going tonight was that name Avril said. Lindsay told me that when a demon is trying to worm its way in to someone's life, it calls itself a 'Pooka'. It's such a nice and friendly sounding name, isn't it?" Avril stirred in her arms and she stroked the child's back and shushed her.

"Didn't they make an old movie about that? With a big rabbit in it or something?"

"Yep. Back around 1950; a real classic. It was called 'Harvey'." Amanda scoffed. "Best PR for the devil in years!"

Julian came through the door holding an empty box that in a previous life had shipped a dozen bottles of chardonnay. While Amanda supervised, he and Paige gathered all of the pieces of the broken stone into it. Together they went out to the end of the dock on the lake. Paige got into the aluminum boat and rowed out to the midpoint. She lowered the box and debris into the lake, filling it with water. When it was full, she released it and watched it sink. She rowed back and they went back to the barn.

Amanda took the gas can and as the others stood at the door she splashed all five gallons along the base of the walls. Returning to the doorway, she told Julian, "Do the honors."

With a glint in his eye that only boys possess, he sparked the lighter and touched the flame to the boards. They ignited immediately, and the four of them edged back, watching as the entire structure became engulfed.

They stayed there until dawn, and went to bed leaving the smoking embers behind.

"Nobody called the Fire Department," Amanda said.

"Yeah..." said Paige. "I didn't even think about it."

"Nobody thought about it," said Julian. His face had that same expression from earlier that night, and his voice the same steady tone of certainty.

"What are we going to tell your father?" Amanda asked.

"He'll be okay."

"You sure?"

Julian's eyes had that funny look again. And in the same voice he said, "Yes. Yes I am."

And then he smiled brightly.

# CHAPTER THIRTY-SIX

## *Three months later...*

T he sweet smell of baking filled Paige's nostrils when she stepped into the house from her day at work. She shrugged out of her coat and slipped the warm leather boots off, looking over through the living room arch where Julian and Avril sat glued to the T.V. watching a Christmas movie. It was the third time this week they were captivated by The Grinch.

She ambled into the room and picked up Avril, planting a big kiss on her cheek. She glanced at the picture of the two kids hanging on the wall. It hung straight as an arrow and she wondered when she'd ever stop checking it whenever she came into the room. Probably never after what they'd gone through.

Julian looked up and flashed a wide grin. "Hi, Aunt Paige. Do you want to build a snow fort after the movie is over?" He sat Yoga style on the floor with Barney's head on his lap, cuddling and petting the dog softly. For his part, Barney wasn't minding the attention at all, his little stump of a tail wagging.

Despite the weariness of putting in an eight-hour shift at the group home, Paige nodded. "Sure." She turned to Avril, "You want to help?"

"Ya! Let's go now!" The little girl's round eyes sparked and she squirmed to get down.

"Hold on a second. I need to get changed and I want to see your mother. Besides, the movie isn't over. You want to see the Grinch give the presents back don't you?" Paige set the excited sprite down on the sofa and turned to go into the kitchen where Amanda was.

Amanda was rinsing the pans and dishes from her baking and smiled when she saw Paige. "How was the driving? Have the snow-plows been out clearing the roads?"

"It's not too bad." She could see the flash of concern in her sister's eyes and added, "The major highways are always cleared first. Josh should be okay driving home." She spotted the plate of chocolate chip cookies and wandered over to the island to take one. She smiled when the warm chocolate melted in her mouth.

Amanda finished the last pan and set it on the rack to rinse. "So...got any plans for tonight? Are you getting together with Matt?"

Paige grinned. "We're having dinner with his aunt Barbara. Do you mind if I take some of these cookies for dessert? They're really good!" She sat down on the stool watching her sister. Amanda was more like the woman she'd once been, full of energy and laughter. There was no indication that she was slipping into depression. The house was resplendent with Christmas decorations, all thanks to Amanda's efforts.

"I'm going to look for an apartment in the New Year. I think it's time that I had my own place. This has been nice, being here with you and the kids but—"

"Oh no! They're going to really miss seeing you every day. Heck, I'll miss it." She wiped her hands and sat down across from Paige.

"Yeah. I'll miss it too." She thought back to their first days in the house, how scared they'd been and how tempted she'd been to convince her sister to just leave. "The house is really nice, Amanda. And especially now at Christmas. It's something right out of Currier and Ives."

Amanda got up and wandered over to the desk perched under the large window. She opened a drawer and scooped out Barbara's red scrapbook. Paige felt a coldness seep through her core. She hadn't thought of the scrapbook since that awful day.

"I've been reading Barbara's entries and all the newspaper clippings. The things that happened here, Elmer Larkspur and then Cora...all the deaths and tragedy that happened on this farm. The years were 1939 and 1968. Barbara makes a good case that a lot of bad things happened in those years. Assassinations and the holocaust. I think we may have dodged another tragedy here, thanks to Barbara and you." She set the book down in front of Paige.

"Actually, I'm glad that you don't want to leave until the New Year. At least get this year behind us. When I read the news on line...all the terrorist attacks, the endless wars. I think we're living in one of those..." Her eyebrows drew tight together, "...what did Barbara call it?"

Paige swallowed hard and she spoke, "Precarious times. Times when the veil separating this world from the next is thin—when bad entities are more easily able to get through." She sighed and her voice was soft when she added, "I think we did our part, don't you?"

"More than anyone would ever know, Sis."

Amanda looked up at her. "More than we'll ever know probably."

Paige chuckled. "I think we know enough, what do you say?"

Amanda giggled in agreement.

Paige got to her feet and placed her hand on her sister's shoulder. "I'm going to get changed so I can take the kids outside to build a snow fort. Want to join us?"

She shook her head. "I've got to get dinner on. Plus, I'm still chilled from this morning out there. You go ahead."

Twenty minutes later Paige and the two kids were bundled up in snow-suits and boots sloughing through the tall drifts of snow that blanketed the lawn. They settled on a spot near the back door to build the snow fort.

"We need to clear a spot for the floor and then built the walls." Paige used the side of her boot to push the snow to the side.

After watching her for a few moments, Julian and Avril mimicked her actions until a spot five feet in diameter had been cleared. Paige knelt down in the snow and began scooping up handfuls, piling them and patting them down on the outer edge. Beside her, Avril's hands in woolly pink mittens worked pushing snow to the wall.

"Hey! C'mon Julian. This fort won't get built with you lolly gagging around." She looked over at the boy who was standing still as a statue looking over to where the barn had been.

Julian had been absolutely right about Josh not being upset over the fire. He didn't ask many questions about it, and never even filed an insurance claim. He told their company that it had been taken down, and they got a reduction in premiums.

His Christmas bonus from his company was going to be more than enough for him to build a nice workshop/man cave in a small barn. He'd been perusing prefab buildings online and was planning on ordering one in the Spring.

"Hey... Jules..." she said softly. "Everything okay?"

"It will be a full moon tonight, Aunt Paige," he said in an even voice.

Another chill went through her. She hadn't heard him speak like that since that night. "Oh?" she said. "Is that important?"

He nodded. "Three moons... yes, it is." He walked over to where the barn had been. They had cleared out all the debris; the only sign it had been there was the bare earth of where the floor had been. It was now snow covered.

"Hey, Julian..." she called.

The boy stepped over to where the center of the building would have been. From the pocket of his coat he withdrew a glass jar. Without having to look closely, Paige knew it was the same vessel Barbara had used the day they cleansed the house.

Mumbling, he poured the water on the ground.

He turned around and came back to where Paige was standing.

"Now," he said, looking up at her with that sweet smile, "now we're done with it all."

### *The End*

# Author's Note

When I was a young girl, around the age of 10, our family was spending a day with friends in the countryside north of Kingston. They had children of their own and one of the sons told us about a home that was abandoned and haunted. Naturally, the rest of us were dying to see it!

It took us over an hour to ride our bicycles out there. It was down at the end of a graveled country laneway. Turning up the drive, you could tell that nobody lived there. The front yard was overgrown and turning wild. It was an older home, unpainted clapboard siding had been turned a bleak grey by weather, and the wrap around veranda was covered in old, dry leaves.

We crept up to the house and peeked in the front windows. In the living room the furniture was coated in dust. The front door was locked, so we creeped around to the back door. Peeking in the kitchen, I saw breakfast dishes still on the table; it was set for two people, including tea cups.

Even though it was a warm summer afternoon, I can recall becoming chilled as we stood peering in the window. One of the children began to speak, and the others shushed him. It was then that one of us mentioned how deathly still it was out there. That phrase, 'deathly still' scared the bejezus out of us and we fled in the glaring cold summer's light.

I never returned to that home at the end of the lane, and now years later, I wouldn't be able to find it. And perhaps that's for the best. Even so, that childhood experience was the seed for this novel.

Thank you for reading my work.  Hopefully, you enjoyed it. If you did, please leave a review on Amazon. Reviews help struggling authors get their books in front of more readers. If for any reason, this book missed the mark for you, please accept my apologies. Hundreds of hours went into its creation and all I can say is "I did my best." If you want to let me know where it fell short, there will be no bad feelings on my part, I promise. I will take your feedback to heart, and try to improve—if not on this one, then certainly on the next.

# OTHER WORKS BY THIS AUTHOR

**Ghost Stories by Michelle Dorey**
The Hauntings Of Kingston
The Haunting Of Crawley House
The Haunted Inn
The Ghosts Of Centre Stree
The Haunting Of Larkspur Farm
The Ghosts Of Hanson House
The Last Laugh

**Paranormal Suspense (The Haunted Ones)**
Haunted Hideout
A Grave Conjuring
Haunted By The Succubus
The Haunted Gathering
The Haunted Reckoning
Graveyard Shift
The Haunted Ghost Tour

**PARANORMAL FANTASY WRITING AS SHELLEY DOREY**
**The Mystical Veil (4 book series)**
Legacy
Heritage
Forsaken
Ascendant

**Celtic Knot (3 book series)**
Song For The God
Immortal Wrath
Mortal Enemies


**PARNORMAL WOMEN'S FICTION BY SHELLEY DOREY**
**Hex After 40 (3 book series)**
The Witching Well
Spellbound
Devil In The Details

**Witch Way (4 book series)**
Midlife Magical Mystery Tour
Hex Appeal
Elf'd Up!
Witchfest

Coming in 2023: The Witches Of Harmony Grove

Printed in Great Britain
by Amazon

28712554R00094